WICKED PLACES

An Ivy Morgan Mystery Book Four

LILY HARPER HART

HarperHart Publications

One

"What are you still doing here?"

Expecting the small Shadow Lake Police Station to be empty this late in the day, Brian Nixon pulled up short when he found his partner Jack Harker still sitting at his desk.

"Thinking," Jack muttered, leaning back in his chair and staring at the ceiling.

"You look like you're about to sit through a root canal," Brian said, moving toward his desk and dropping a file on the corner. "You're about to go on vacation – one you've handsomely earned, mind you. I expected you to be out of here already. You have nine days in a row off, son. Start enjoying them."

Jack was a recent transplant to Shadow Lake, a small hamlet located in the northwestern portion of Michigan's lower peninsula. He'd only been in town a few months, but his camping trip with his college buddies had been on the calendar since he was hired. Brian couldn't figure out why Jack – who had been looking forward to his vacation – was so morose.

"I'm not sure I want to go," Jack admitted, tearing his gaze away from the ceiling and focusing on Brian. "Maybe I should cancel my trip."

Brian pressed his lips together in an attempt to keep from laughing, but failed and caused Jack to scowl when he loudly guffawed. "Do you want to know what your real problem is?"

"Not really," Jack replied, irritated.

"Your real problem is that when you planned this little outing – and no offense, but you don't strike me as a camping sort of a guy, so I'm worried you're going to get lost in the woods and we'll never hear from you again – you didn't have a girlfriend," Brian volunteered. "Now you have a girlfriend and you haven't been separated from her for weeks – not even a single night – and you're rethinking your trip because you don't want to be away from her."

Jack dramatically rolled his eyes. "I am perfectly capable of being away from Ivy for a week. I'm not some ... wimp ... who can't live without his girlfriend for a few days."

Ivy Morgan was Shadow Lake's version of nirvana, at least if you listened to every man in her age group wax poetic about her during outings to the local bar. She was certainly Jack's version of nirvana. After fighting the witchy woman's wiles for weeks, Jack finally gave in and admitted he didn't want to go another day without her. They'd been inseparable ever since.

They fought like cats and dogs – engaging in actual screaming matches because each one of them thought the other was overly bossy – but that only led to heavy petting and cuddling minutes later (and a few other things). They were passion and poutiness wrapped up in a pretty package, and Brian couldn't help but sneer at Jack's statement.

"I think it's good you and Ivy are spending time apart," Brian said, changing tactics.

Jack cocked a challenging eyebrow. "You do?"

"I know quite a few men who want to give her a call now that she's dating, and they're afraid to do it when you're around because they think you'll go all Hulk on them," Brian said. "This will give Ivy a chance to explore her options."

"I hate you sometimes," Jack muttered, rolling his neck until it cracked. "Fine. Do you want to hear me say it?"

Brian crossed his arms over his chest and waited.

"I can't go that long without seeing her," Jack admitted, his expression rueful. "I'm a wimp."

"Oh, you're breaking my heart," Brian deadpanned. "You know there's a solution to this problem, right?"

"What?"

"You could ask Ivy to go with you," Brian replied. "She knows how to camp. In fact, she's pretty good at it."

"I can't do that," Jack protested.

"Why not?"

"Because I'm leaving the day after tomorrow and she'll take me asking her at the last minute as an insult," Jack said. "Plus, well, I haven't told my college buddies that I'm even dating someone. That will come out while we're camping and Ivy's feelings will be hurt."

"You haven't even been dating Ivy a month yet," Brian pointed out. "She's not so irrational that would set her off. If you want to know the truth, I have an inkling her feelings are already hurt because you didn't invite her."

Jack stilled, worried. "What do you mean?"

"Jack, you told me that your buddies are all bringing their wives and girlfriends," Brian said. "How do you think it makes Ivy feel knowing she's the only one who wasn't invited?"

"But ... crap," Jack muttered, pressing the heel of his hand against his forehead. "I didn't think of that. I didn't want her to think I was pressuring her so I didn't ask, even though I wanted to ask."

"It's not too late."

"She has a business," Jack reminded his partner. "She can't walk away from the nursery for an entire week with no notice. It's not even fair to ask."

"Michael can handle running the nursery," Brian said, referring to Ivy's father. "He works there five days a week. I'm sure he wouldn't have a problem with it."

"What about her cat?"

Brian knew Jack was grasping for excuses because he was terrified of asking Ivy to go camping with him. It was a ridiculous fear from Brian's perspective, but Jack and Ivy were so passionately fiery he could understand his partner's trepidation. He just couldn't accept it.

"Doesn't Max watch that cat whenever necessary? It's a cat. It's not a kid you're foisting on someone for a week."

As Ivy's brother, Max had been roped into watching her cat numerous times – including a few weeks before when Jack and Ivy took off on an impromptu road trip to Detroit to investigate a case.

Jack sighed, resigned. "She's going to be upset when I ask her."

"Would you rather be a coward and not ask her and have a rotten time camping, or would you rather swallow your pride and ask her and have a great time with everyone?"

Jack pushed himself to his feet. "Okay."

"What are you going to do?" Brian asked, feigning curiosity.

"I'm going to go and beg my girl to go camping with me."

"That's what I thought you were going to do," Brian said, watching Jack shuffle out of the department with a small smile. "Have a good vacation."

IVY MORGAN LEANED BACK AND STUDIED THE SECTION OF HER flower garden she'd just weeded with a frown on her pretty face. She usually enjoyed working in her garden. She found it relaxing and rewarding at the same time. Today was a different story.

She never pictured herself as a petulant or clingy person, but the idea of her new boyfriend going camping without her – when other wives and girlfriends were going to be present – bothered her. She couldn't explain it.

Sure, Jack and Ivy had been inseparable for weeks – and she'd enjoyed every moment of it – but she didn't understand why he needed time away from her so soon after they got together. The idea that she was acting like a needy female – something she loathed – bothered her as much as her hurt feelings regarding the camping trip.

She had no idea what was wrong with her.

She turned when she heard a vehicle pulling into the driveway behind her, forcing a pleasant smile for Jack's benefit as she watched him park and hop out of his truck. She was determined to send him on his way with happy feelings – and wait to pout until he was out of town and could really wallow in her self-pity without an audience.

"Hey, honey," Jack said, moving to Ivy's side and dropping a kiss on her perfectly pink lips. "What are you doing over here? I thought for sure you'd be at the nursery."

"I was over there most of the day," Ivy said, dusting off her knees. "My dad likes it when I leave him in charge. He says it makes him feel like king of the nursery. Plus, he was bugging me, so I had to get away. He said he would close up."

"That's good," Jack said, gripping his hands together. If Ivy didn't know better she would think he was nervous.

"How was your last day before your vacation?"

"Dull," Jack replied, his face unreadable as he watched Ivy's profile. "I … how was your day?"

"I just told you how my day was," Ivy answered, swiveling. "What's your deal? You're acting … weird."

"How?" Jack asked, his temper flaring. "I haven't done one weird thing since I got here."

"You're about to rip your own hands off," Ivy countered, pointing for emphasis. "If you say nothing is wrong, though, who am I to judge? What do you want for dinner? I was thinking of cooking a nice stir fry."

"That sounds good," Jack said, following Ivy up the steps and into her small cottage. The abode was homey and warm – just like Ivy was most days – but it was also bohemian and charming. He loved spending time with her there. "Can we talk a second?"

Ivy froze, her shoulders stiffening at the tone of his words. "Are you walking away?"

Jack scowled. He hated it when she naturally assumed he was going to leave her. It was the furthest thing from his mind. He didn't blame her for her suspicions and reservations – he'd been forthcoming when he told her he wasn't looking for a relationship when he first came to town – but it still annoyed him that she always jumped to that conclusion.

"Stop asking that," Jack hissed. "I'm not going anywhere. I … it drives me crazy when you assume I'm going to walk out on you. I promised you I wasn't going to do that."

"Fine," Ivy said, holding her hands up in a placating manner. "I apologize. You are going somewhere, though. You're going camping." *Without me*, she silently added. "Can we not fight? We only have tomorrow together before you take off."

"That's what I want to talk about," Jack hedged, his eyes darting around the room as he avoided her pointed gaze. "I don't want to go without you."

Ivy lifted her eyebrows, surprised. "Since when?"

"Since ... since we got together," Jack responded. "I kind of lost track of everything over the past few weeks. Between fighting, getting together, fighting some more, and then that whole ghost possession thing ... I forgot about the camping trip until it was already upon me."

Ivy tugged on her limited patience as she watched Jack struggle. She never wanted to cause him pain. The past few weeks had been busy for the duo, his former partner's murderous spirit taking over a woman's body to stalk them. She didn't blame him for losing track of the camping trip.

"It's okay, Jack," Ivy said. "You don't need to feel like you have to invite me. I understand. You haven't seen your friends in a long time."

"Oh, don't do that," Jack countered, wagging a finger in Ivy's face. "I don't *have* to invite you. I *want* to invite you. I've wanted to invite you since I remembered the camping trip.

"The problem is, I spent the first few days after that worrying it was too soon for us to go camping with my old friends because I didn't want you to feel uncomfortable," he continued. "Then I felt like an idiot for not asking you right away and I kept letting it go because I convinced myself you were going to say no."

"I see."

Jack made a face, her feigned disinterest squeezing his heart. "Would you have agreed to come with me if I asked?"

"Yes."

"That's what Brian said," Jack lamented. "I ... do you want to come camping with me?"

"Do you really want me to go camping with you, or are you only asking because you think you should do it in an attempt not to hurt my feelings?"

"We are completely dysfunctional when it comes to conversations like this," Jack muttered. "The truth is, I don't want to be away from you. It makes me sound like a wimp, but there it is.

"I would love to introduce you to my friends, but now I'm really worried if you say yes you're only doing it to appease me," he said.

Ivy wanted to string him along a little bit longer, but he looked so miserable she couldn't bring herself to do it. "I want to go camping with you," she said finally. "I don't want you to feel obligated to ask me, though."

"You know what? I want you to go camping with me and you want to go. We're not continuing this conversation so we can both feel like … ."

"Jackholes?" Ivy supplied.

"You know I hate it when you use my name like that," Jack muttered.

Ivy took pity on him and reached over so she could grab his hand. "I would love to go camping with you."

"You could've said that five minutes ago and eased off on the mental torture," Jack growled, tugging her to him so he could hug her. "I always want to spend time with you, honey. Please don't ever worry about that."

Ivy rested her head against Jack's strong chest. "I like spending time with you, too."

"We need to work on our communication skills."

"I'd rather keep doing what we're doing and have sex whenever we have an argument."

Jack barked out a laugh and pressed a kiss to her forehead. "You really are my favorite person in the world. You know that, right?"

"The feeling is mutual."

Two

"I don't have a problem with it," Michael Morgan said, rolling his eyes as his only daughter talked to him like he was a teenager being left alone without parental supervision for the first time. "I promise not to have any wild parties while you're out of town, *Mom*."

Ivy made a face. She loved her father beyond reason. He still gave her headaches on a regular basis. "That's not what I meant and you know it!"

Max Morgan sat on the counter in front of Ivy's plant nursery and broke into raucous guffaws. "I think we should throw an out-of-control kegger while Ivy is off playing kissy-face with Jack."

"You know I'm right here, right?" Jack asked, flicking Max's ear and sending him a warning look. "I can hear you when you say things like that."

"I wasn't trying to be subtle," Max replied, returning the ear flick and smirking when Jack tried to grab his wrist and missed.

"I'm not trying to tell you what to do, Dad," Ivy said, adjusting her tone. "I just … it's last minute, and if you can't run the nursery for the entire week then I'll shut it down. It's not a big deal."

"Wait a second," Jack said, pushing himself away from the counter.

"That doesn't seem fair. If your dad can't do it, we won't go. I don't want you missing out on money because I didn't ask in a timely fashion."

"You can't skip your camping trip," Ivy argued. "You've had this planned since before you came to town. You're going."

"I'm not going without you," Jack shot back, crossing his arms over his chest.

"You're such a woman," Max teased, reaching forward so he could flick Jack's ear again and earning a murderous look when he almost toppled off the counter. "Do you think you'll die if you don't see Ivy for a week?"

"I think you're going to die if you don't shut up," Jack warned.

"Boys, knock it off," Michael ordered, shaking his head. "I thought Ivy and Max arguing when they were teenagers was bad. You two are … really annoying." He turned his attention back to Ivy. "I promise to run things how you like them and that everything will be fine. I think a break from work for a week will do you good. You love camping."

"I do love camping," Ivy conceded. "I feel guilty about dumping my problems on you, though."

"I take off six months of every year to go to Florida," Michael reminded her. "I like being here. It doesn't feel like work because I love people and like to talk about plants. Everything is going to be fine."

"Yeah, Ivy," Max chided. "Are you saying you don't have faith in your own father? What kind of daughter are you?"

"You really want me to beat you, don't you?" Jack asked.

"I work out five times a week," Max replied. "I think I could take you."

"I've already proven that you can't," Jack shot back, reminding Max of an earlier incident when Max thought Jack was a prowler stalking Ivy. "Don't push me."

"You've lost all the fun in your personality since you started dating my sister," Max said. "You're just like her now. You know that, right?"

"Wait a second, are you saying I'm not fun?" Ivy asked, swiveling so she could take on Max. "I'll have you know that I'm tons of fun. Tell him I'm fun, Dad."

"Max, your sister is fun," Michael replied dryly.

"Ivy, before Jack came around you were one step away from being the town recluse," Max said. "I don't ever remember anyone calling you fun."

"She's tons of fun," Jack argued. "Leave her alone."

"I don't like that you're always on Ivy's side," Max said. "I'm her brother. You should be on my side occasionally if you want me to stand up for you when she gets angry again, because we all know that's going to happen on a regular basis."

"She's cuter."

Max rolled his eyes. "I'll have you know that I'm considered the hot one in the family."

"Only in your own mind," Jack said.

"Knock it off you two," Michael said. "You're giving me a migraine."

"Join the club," Ivy muttered.

"Ivy, I promise this is going to be okay," Michael said. "I'll take over the nursery, your brother will take care of Nicodemus, and everything is going to be great. Enjoy camping. You've earned it."

"Thank you," Ivy said, offering her father an impulsive hug.

Michael patted Ivy's back as he returned the embrace. "You haven't been camping in a long time," he said after a moment. "I hope you're not rusty."

"I'm sure it's like riding a bike," Ivy said, pulling away from her father. "I can't wait. I think I need to run to the outdoor supply store to pick up a few things, though. Jack, how much stuff do you have?"

When Ivy shifted her attention to Jack she found a quizzical expression on his face.

"What stuff?" Jack asked, confused. "I got a sleeping bag, bug spray, and a cooler. Isn't that all I need?"

Ivy faltered. "Have you ever been camping before?"

Max snickered. "He's a city boy. I don't think he's ever been camping."

"I've slept under the stars," Jack protested. "My mother used to let me have a campout in the back yard once a year. It's the same thing."

"We're going camping for a week," Ivy pointed out.

"I know."

"Oh, this is going to be priceless," Max intoned. "Jack has no idea what he's doing and Ivy is the bossiest camper ever. I see many a fight in your future, kids."

Max's words irked Ivy, and yet she had a feeling he was right. "I think we should go to the store together," she said, choosing her words carefully. "It wouldn't hurt to look over a few things … just to be sure we have everything covered, mind you."

Jack wasn't fooled by Ivy's diplomatic approach. "You think I'm clueless, don't you?"

"I think you're very handsome."

Jack blew out a sigh, the possibility of fighting before they even hit the campground frustrating him. "Let's pick out camping supplies, honey."

"You won't regret it," Ivy said, reaching for his hand as enthusiasm washed over her. "I love shopping for camping supplies."

Jack couldn't help but enjoy her excitement. "Let's do it."

"I WANT a purple one," Ivy said an hour later, pointing at the bottom shelf so Jack knew which sleeping bag to grab.

"Is there a rule about what color sleeping bag you need to survive in the woods?" Jack teased, grabbing the item in question and tossing it into their cart.

"I just like the color."

"I think you should get pink to match your hair," Jack said, affectionately tugging on a strand of Ivy's hair. It was long and brown, pink streaks weaving through the rich color. "I happen to love your hair, so if you're in a pink sleeping bag I'll know which one to sneak into in the middle of the night when we're sleeping under the stars."

Ivy pressed her lips together as she regarded Jack. She didn't want him to think she was taking over his camping trip, but she also wanted to make sure they had a good time. "I have a suggestion," she said, hoping she sounded tactful. "Now, if what I'm about to say upsets you, tell me right away and I'll shut my mouth."

"You're about to tell me I have no idea what I'm doing, aren't you?"

"I'm about to tell you that sleeping under the stars is a very romantic notion," Ivy replied. "It's also completely impractical. We need a tent."

Jack frowned. "I want to sleep under the stars," he protested. "I have visions of you and me snuggling together in the same sleeping bag when everyone else isn't looking."

"We can snuggle under the stars as much as you want," Ivy clarified. "We still need a tent. We can get one with a roof that opens."

"But ... ."

Ivy pressed her hand to Jack's chest to still him. "Just listen to me for a second, okay?"

Jack narrowed his eyes and nodded.

"What happens if it rains?"

"I ... huh." Jack rubbed the back of his neck. "Well, we can sit in my truck until the rain passes."

"What if it rains for an entire day?"

"I ... ." Jack made a disgusted sound in the back of his throat. "Fine. We can get a tent."

"It's not just rain, Jack," Ivy said. "We need a place to change our clothes, too. Most of these campgrounds have bathroom facilities, but you wouldn't believe what a pain it is to constantly go there when you have to change your clothes."

"I was just going to get dressed by the campfire."

"You were going to get naked in front of your friends' wives and girlfriends?" Ivy asked, dubious.

"No! I was just going to change my shorts. I'll be wearing boxer shorts."

"The same ones for a week straight?"

"Huh," Jack mused, tilting his head to the side as he realized his mistake. "Wow. It's a good thing I invited you, honey. I would've turned this trip into a disaster in five minutes flat."

Ivy smiled as she rolled to the balls of her feet and pressed a soft kiss to Jack's cheek. "There's another reason we need the tent."

"I'm listening."

"As much fun as cuddling under the stars sounds in theory, bugs are a real issue and so is the cold," Ivy said. "If we have a tent, we can zipper both of our sleeping bags together and make a big enough sleeping area that we can … um … make up on a regular basis."

Jack grinned. He couldn't help himself. Since they fought so often – and felt the need to jump each other minutes after – they'd taken to referring to sex bouts after fights as "making up."

"You are the smartest woman in the world, Ivy Morgan," Jack said, cupping the back of her head and planting a smoldering kiss on her. "Is it wrong I'm already looking forward to making up?"

"You're not the only one," Ivy said, turning her attention back to the tents. "I think we should get this one. It's tall enough in the center for you to stand up – almost – and it's wide enough that we can keep all our stuff inside and spread the sleeping bags out beneath the window so you can sleep under the stars."

"You had me at making up, honey," Jack said, grabbing the tent and dropping it in their basket. "What else do we need?"

"You seem eager to spend money," Ivy teased.

"I've realized that I'm woefully unprepared for what's ahead," Jack countered. "I grew up in the suburbs of Detroit. The only woods we had consisted of the strip of trees between minimarts."

"You're cute," Ivy said, slipping her hand into his as he pushed the shopping cart to the next aisle.

"I'm not joking," Jack said. "If this was a movie, I would be the first one to die in the zombie apocalypse because I don't know how to survive without electricity."

"I guess it's good you have me then."

"I think that every day," Jack said, his eyes flashing with earnest honesty before returning to their flirty game. "What else do we need?"

"We need two flashlights and a lantern," Ivy said, grabbing the items and dropping them into the cart. "We also need a few citronella candles, a pot and a pan for cooking, and probably a trip to the grocery store."

"Can't I just bring a pot and pan from my kitchen?" Jack asked.

"Only if you want them to melt in the fire," Ivy replied, unruffled. "We need cast iron cookware. Think of it as an investment for future camping trips."

"Honey, my idea of camping is rolling around with you under the stars in your back yard," Jack said. "Pots and pans it is, though. I'm deferring to you because you're the only one who is going to be able to help me survive the zombie apocalypse."

"Do you care if I put some vegetarian stuff in your cooler?" Ivy asked, grabbing two metal prongs so they could roast marshmallows.

"No," Jack scoffed. "Ivy, you don't have to ask about stuff like that. You know that, right?"

Ivy shrugged, noncommittal. "Some guys don't like it when women assume they can take over things," she said. "I'm trying really hard not to be bossy."

"I'll be really thankful if you do that in front of my friends," Jack said. "I'm already going to look like an idiot because you're going to have to teach me to do things. That doesn't mean I'm going to be upset if you put stuff in my cooler. Why would you think that?"

"I ... ." Ivy broke off, biting her lip.

"This would be an example of the communication we need to work on," Jack prodded.

"I guess I'm worried that I'm going to somehow ... chase you off ... if I get too proprietary," Ivy admitted, hating the rush of heat that climbed her cheeks. "Men don't like demanding women."

"Well, honey, I happened to fall for you because you were demanding ... and bossy ... and really cute in your skirt and bare feet at a murder scene," Jack said. "I'm not going anywhere, Ivy. I know I messed up – a few times – but I promise I'm not going to break your heart. Not again. Please, if you don't believe anything else, believe that."

"I do believe that," Ivy said. "I just ... I can't remember being this happy in a really long time. That usually means something awful is going to happen."

Jack drew Ivy to him so he could tilt her chin up and study her face. "If something bad happens, it will not involve me leaving – especially because you put food in my cooler, or bossed me around, or made me look like a fool while camping."

Ivy's smile was sheepish. "I sound like a needy chick. I hate that."

"We're going to have fun," Jack said. "We've got a whole week in front of us where we get to sleep under the stars and ... stab each other with those long forks you picked out. It's going to be fine. It's going to be an adventure."

Ivy rolled her eyes. "Those are for roasting marshmallows so we can make s'mores."

"See, it's good you're coming with me," Jack said, slinging an arm over her shoulders as they continued to move down the aisle. "I would starve to death without you."

"And be very sad because you would have to sleep alone at night," Ivy added.

"Oh, well, that's a given," Jack said. "I can't wait to see how you're going to poke your feet out of the bottom of a sleeping bag."

"I'm sure I'll figure something out."

"You're nothing if not talented," Jack agreed.

Three

"I'm glad we're the first ones here," Ivy said, hopping out of Jack's truck on the first day of their camping trip and glancing around. "That will allow us to pick the best spot for our tent."

"It's not a competition, honey," Jack said, following her to the back of his truck so they could start unpacking. "For the record, though, I'm glad we're here first, too. This way I can watch you put up the tent and take credit for it when they all get here."

Ivy smirked. Jack was taking his camping deficiencies in stride and was eager to learn. He'd watched her ready bags of food for hours the previous day, content to let her plan their menu and figure out exactly what they would need for their week of fun and relaxation.

In the back of his brain, Jack always worried Ivy's vegetarianism would come back to bite him at mealtimes. In truth, she always went out of her way to make sure he had something to enjoy. He hadn't been surprised when she packed hot dogs, hamburgers, and steaks for him. In fact, he'd been thankful … and a little awed at the pragmatic way her mind worked.

"Okay," Ivy said, taking charge as she looked around the area. "According to the information they sent you we have these three camp-sites. Two of your friends have campers, right?"

Jack nodded. "They made fun of me because I didn't have a camper."

"That's the wimpy way to camp, honey," Ivy said. "You're going to be happy we're doing it our way."

"You mean *your* way," Jack corrected, although he winked to let her know he was joking.

"Okay, smart guy, why don't you pick the spot for our tent?" Ivy suggested, her hands landing on her narrow hips.

Jack pursed his lips at the challenge. He loved riling her up. "Fine," he said, brushing off his hands and moving away from the truck so he could scan the campsites. "I think we should go over there," he said, pointing at the slot on the right.

"Why?"

"Because ... I always sleep in the right side of the bed."

Ivy wanted to maintain a serious façade, but she couldn't stop herself from laughing. "It's a good thing you're handsome," she said. "I think we should put the campers on either end, thus creating kind of a wall to block other people off, and the tents in the center where we'll probably have most of the bonfires."

"You're good at this," Jack said, tweaking her nose. "Of course, you're good at everything. I really shouldn't be surprised."

"You're trying to be charming because you want me to put up the tent so we can have a few hours alone before your friends show up," Ivy said. "Admit it."

"There's absolutely no reason to deny it."

"I like the way your mind works," Ivy said, grabbing Jack's face and planting a sloppy kiss on him. "I think we should take the spot closest to the end of the slot so we can be buffered by the trees and also look out at the water. I can position the tent so when we open the flaps we'll have a lake view."

Jack grinned. "Now I like the way your mind works," he said, grabbing her before she could wander away and kissing her senseless. When they separated, Ivy instinctively tidied her hair and Jack tugged a restless hand through his. "Get that tent up."

"Yes, sir," Ivy said, kicking her heels together as she mock saluted. "Is there anything else you want me to do, sir?"

"Not until you get that tent up."

The couple set about their tasks, Jack carrying everything to the location Ivy picked for their tent while she unpacked the box and placed all the items on the ground to study them. When he was done, he watched her with unbridled fascination as she slapped everything together without even glancing at the instructions.

"I wouldn't even have the box open yet," Jack admitted.

"You're out of your element," Ivy said. "You'll still have fun, and I won't say a word when you take credit for putting up the tent."

"Did you camp a lot when you were younger?" Jack asked, stretching his long legs out in front of him as he leaned back on the picnic table bench.

"You know my parents," Ivy said. "They've always been nature freaks. They instilled that in Max and me when were young. I always remember going camping at least twice every summer.

"Max loved it because he liked to catch snakes and walk around with them in his pockets so he could freak people out," she continued. "I love animals, but snakes ... I'm not going to lie, they give me nightmares."

"I'm not a fan of snakes or bugs," Jack said. "You're still braver than me."

"You're the bravest person I know, Jack," Ivy countered. "Camping doesn't make you brave. It's just a hobby. What you do every single day when you put on your badge is a lot braver than camping."

"If you're trying to stroke my ego, it's working," Jack said, grinning.

"You're going to be fine, Jack," Ivy said. "We can take hikes together ... and go kayaking ... and if all the outdoors living becomes too hard to handle, we can always go into town for dinner."

"I don't know anything about this area," Jack said. "The closest town is called Gaylord, right? What can you tell me about it?"

Ivy shrugged. "It used to be a lot smaller," she explained. "There's not a lot of shopping around here, so when we were younger and my mother decided she needed to stock up on things we either had to go with her to Gaylord or Traverse City."

"It seems fairly big for this area now," Jack said. "We should come over here for dinner one night."

"We should go to the Mexican place," Ivy suggested, feeding a long pole into a nylon sleeve. "It's called La Señorita, and the green salsa is to die for."

"I'll make sure we get over there one night this week," Jack promised. "I'm sure we'll want a night to ourselves at some point."

"We should go to Call of the Wild, too."

"What's Call of the Wild?"

"It's this hilarious museum full of dead animals and they're put in outdoor scenes with narration."

Jack knit his eyebrows together. "You want to look at dead animals? Why don't I believe that?"

"The animals weren't murdered," Ivy replied. "Some were hit by cars and most have been dead for a very long time. They even have a polar bear. Besides, while the museum is kitschy and fun, it's the gift shop that is the best thing there."

"Why is that?"

"It's like an out-of-control flea market with a lot of weird stuff that you just can't find anyplace else."

"Well, I'm sold," Jack said. "We'll do both of those things."

"We're here to see your friends," Ivy reminded him, moving to the next side of the tent and feeding another pole through the nylon. "Don't you want to spend time with them?"

"I want to spend *some* time with them," Jack clarified. "I want to spend a lot of time with you."

"You're going to get really lucky in a few minutes, Jack," Ivy said.

"I'm looking forward to it," Jack said, licking his lips and trying to force his mind toward something innocuous as Ivy worked. "Did you ever come here camping when you were younger?"

"A few times," Ivy answered. "My mom loved this place because of the lake. She loves to kayak. I was always scared because of the Bigfoot stories."

Jack stilled, curiosity warring with the need to laugh. "Bigfoot?"

"Sasquatch … the dogman … werewolves … you know, Bigfoot," Ivy pressed. "This entire area is full of Bigfoot legends."

"Oh, well, you're going to have to expand on that," Jack chuckled. "I need to hear about Bigfoot."

"It's not technically Bigfoot," Ivy clarified. "It's … upright canines."

"How is that different?"

"Fine. It's Bigfoot," Ivy said, rolling her eyes. "If you make fun of me, I'm not getting in this tent with you before your friends show up. You've been warned."

"I'm not going to make fun of you," Jack said. "I just … I love stories like this. I know you were a kid when you were frightened. I'm not going to be a … ."

"Jackhole?" Ivy challenged.

Jack scowled. "We're coming up with a new word for that this week whether you like it or not."

Ivy giggled. "Okay, so there have been reports about upright canines in this area for a really long time," she said. "Supposedly the stories go back as far as when settlers first moved to Michigan.

"I don't know if those sightings were real, but somewhere around the 1930s the sightings increased and it became a state legend," she continued.

"I've never heard of this legend."

"That's because you grew up in Detroit and you had real monsters on every corner to fight."

"Good point," Jack said. "Go on. I find this fascinating."

"Depending on what you believe – and I know you don't believe, so there's no reason to be a pain – people have claimed sightings of the dogman for years," Ivy said. "Most people in the state refer to him that way rather than Bigfoot, just FYI."

"I've got it."

"The first one I remember hearing about happened at Dead Man's Hill over in the Jordan River Valley," Ivy said. "It's by a small town called Mancelona. We should really go there for a hike one day when the leaves start turning in the fall. I promise you've never seen anything more beautiful."

"I've seen you and you're more beautiful," Jack said. "The hike sounds nice, though. Go back to Bigfoot."

Ivy made an exasperated sound in the back of her throat. "Anyway, someone claimed they were hiking around the Dead Man's Hill area and they saw a big ... dogman ... walking through the words. It was a woman, and she claimed she had a photo. It was pretty blurry, and my parents were convinced it was actually a bear.

"Later that night everyone told stories about when they'd seen a dogman – these are rational people, mind you – and there were so many of them I got a little anxious," she continued. "Two people – they were friends of my parents – claimed they saw the dogman when they were camping here, and we happened to be here at the time so I was a nervous wreck."

"You've never seen Bigfoot, right?"

"Don't push me, Jack," Ivy warned, getting to her feet. "Can you please move to that side of the tent and help me?"

Jack wordlessly did as instructed, his eyes never leaving Ivy's face. "I'm waiting for you to finish the story."

"There's not much to tell," Ivy said, pointing so Jack would know what to do as they lifted the poles into place and secured them at the bottom of the domed tent. "A lot of people around here have a story about the dogman, just like a lot of people in New Mexico have a story about aliens. It is what it is."

"You're leaving something out," Jack prodded, watching as Ivy grabbed the metal hooks to anchor the tent to the ground before moving to help. "Why were you freaked out?"

"Wait, we need to turn the tent so the door is that way," Ivy said, helping Jack maneuver it to the right position. "If you must know, Max took advantage of how scared I was by the stories and dressed up with leaves and stuff all over him and jumped out of the bushes and scared the crap out of me when I was walking to the bathroom one night.

"I screamed and ran to my father," she continued. "I was so worked up I actually slept in their tent that night."

"Max needs a good beating," Jack said.

"He thought it was funny."

"Oh, it's funny, but you're my girl now and I'll wrestle him down and make him apologize next time we see him," Jack said. "I will also thank him, because I'm hopeful this dogman fear will mean you sleep on top of me in the tent."

Ivy snickered. "You're a piece of work," she said. "Let's get the cushion I brought and put the sleeping bags together. Then we can ... stare at the lake and bond."

"That only sounds fun if we're naked."

"That's the plan," Ivy said, grabbing one side of the large cushion she'd thought to grab out of the nursery and helping Jack carry it to the tent. They situated it in the middle of the floor and then Ivy went to work zipping the sleeping bags together while Jack carried the rest of their belongings inside.

Once they were settled, Jack flopped on the cushion and sighed. "I thought we were wimping out when you suggested the cushion, but this is the best idea ever," he said. "It's soft. Where did you get it?"

"It's from my parents' old camping trailer," Ivy replied, rolling to her side so she could snuggle closer and resting her chin on his chest. "I took it when they sold the camper and I'm glad I did. We're going to be comfortable in here."

Jack brushed Ivy's hair away from her face and kissed the side of her mouth. "Plus, it's a cushion," he said. "It won't make noise when we ... dream about the dogman."

"I'm never telling you anything again," Ivy complained.

"I like hearing stories about you when you were little," Jack said, refusing to let her pull away from him. "I can just picture you getting even with Max."

"Oh, I got even," Ivy said. "I made him think the basement was haunted by using a rake to scratch on the windows and he slept on the living room floor for two weeks straight."

Jack barked out a laugh. "That's my girl."

Ivy shifted her contemplative blue eyes to his angular face. "How long until your friends show up?"

Jack checked his watch. "We have at least an hour."

"I think you'd better get to wowing me then," Ivy teased. "I don't want you to run out of time."

Jack barked as he rolled on top of her, panting like a dog as he tugged his shirt off. "Don't worry, this dogman won't terrify you. I will, however, expect to be petted accordingly when I'm done."

"Bring it on."

Four

J ack and Ivy got so carried away with their game – and Jack's incessant need to bark throughout the romantic interlude – they lost track of time and fell asleep. Ivy curled her arm around Jack's chest as he held her close – neither one bothering to cover themselves under the bright sun as it cascaded through the roof of their tent – and dozed off before they realized what was happening.

That's exactly how Jack's friends found them an hour and a half later.

"I see you're taking to camping better than I expected, Jack," one of the men said, his wolfish grin the first thing Ivy saw when she wrenched her eyes open. "I can see why."

"Holy crud," Ivy said, reaching for her discarded clothes to cover herself as Jack blocked her body with his by sitting up.

It took Jack a moment to realize that six sets of curious eyes were fixed on him through the open flap at the end of the tent. "Get out," Jack ordered, reality washing over him. "Don't stare at us."

"We'll be unpacking and getting settled. Come and join us when you're ready."

Jack watched them go, their laughter simultaneously amusing and irritating him. He rolled his eyes until they landed on a mortified Ivy. "I'm so sorry, honey."

Instead of yelling and screaming like he expected, Ivy broke out in raucous laughter and buried her face in her hands. "That is not how I envisioned meeting them."

"The good news is that you just made the best first impression ever," Jack said. "The bad news is that I'm going to have to kill all of them for seeing you naked."

"I'm not sure how much they saw," Ivy countered. "I was kind of … crushed … against you."

"That's exactly how I like you to sleep," Jack said, grabbing the back of her neck and kissing her. "I'm sorry about that, though. I didn't mean to fall asleep."

"I think you wore yourself out with all that barking."

"Trust me, honey, that's not what wore me out," Jack said, smiling as he released her. "Come on and get dressed. I'll introduce you to everyone. They're going to love you – although I'm fairly certain some of them already do."

It took Jack and Ivy about ten minutes to get situated, Ivy insisting on running a brush through her hair while Jack watched with a wide smile. Once she was ready, Jack linked his fingers with hers and led her out of the tent, widening his eyes as he watched his friends toil with metal beams that appeared to mechanically lower toward the ground at the front of their campers.

"What are they doing?"

Ivy smiled. She loved that Jack seemed so uncertain regarding camping. He was usually sure of himself in almost every situation. She found his confusion cute. "They're balancing the campers."

"It looks … difficult."

"I'm sure they know what they're doing," Ivy said, squeezing his hand. "Do you want to introduce me, or are you afraid I'm going to embarrass you because they've seen me naked?"

"Oh, honey, there's nothing embarrassing about you when you're naked," Jack said, locking gazes with her. "That's the most glorious thing ever."

"So cute," Ivy said, pinching his cheek and jiggling it.

Jack wrinkled his nose. "I wish they weren't here so I could drag you right back into that tent."

"We'll have plenty of time for that," Ivy said. "It looks like your friends with the tent are thinking ahead and pitching their tent on the other side of the campsite." Ivy pointed and Jack watched his friend struggle with the nylon contraption.

"Do you think I should help?" Jack asked.

"No. Then they'll know you didn't put up our tent."

"Ha, ha," he intoned, gripping her hand. "Come on. I'll make introductions."

For the first time since Jack suggested she join him on his camping trip, Ivy was nervous. What if they didn't like her? What if they took one look at her pink hair and thought Jack had lost his mind? What if they tried to talk Jack out of dating her?

In her heart, Ivy knew Jack was committed to the relationship. They'd had issues with communication at certain points, but she believed him when he said he wanted to be with her. He struggled with doubt after meeting her, the same way she did when she first laid eyes on him. They overcame that, and Ivy was happy. Now her biggest worry was something coming along that would torpedo that happiness.

"Well, there he is," the man working on the tent said, straightening. "I'm glad to see you found your clothes before you joined us. Otherwise that might have been embarrassing."

Jack rolled his eyes but extended his hand and greeted his friend. "Alex. How are things?"

"They're good," Alex replied, his eyes twinkling as they shifted to Ivy. "I see things are good with you, too."

"They're definitely good," Jack said, moving Ivy in front of him. "Alex and Maria Scully, this is Ivy Morgan."

"It's nice to meet you," Ivy said, slipping her hand in Alex's to shake it and offering Maria a pleasant smile.

"It's nice to meet you, too," Alex said, vigorously shaking Ivy's hand before releasing it. "It would've been nicer if we knew you existed so we could've prepared ourselves for that ... wonderful moment at your tent."

Ivy faltered. "I ... ."

"That's my fault," Jack said, stepping in smoothly. "We've been extremely busy and I forgot all about the camping trip until you sent that email reminding everyone a week ago."

"Have you two only been dating for a week?" Alex challenged, lifting an eyebrow. "That's not how it looked to me."

"We've been dating for a few weeks," Jack replied, not missing a beat. "We've been ... verbally sparring ... a few more weeks. Don't give her a hard time."

"I was just joking," Alex said, making an exaggerated face. "I'm just ... surprised. You haven't had a girlfriend in a long time – well, at least one you've brought around us."

"I haven't had anyone I've cared enough about to bring around you in a long time," Jack said. "Ivy is special."

"I can see Ivy is special," Alex said. "Now I know why you're selling your house downstate and moving up here for good. I was wondering, and now I know why."

Ivy shifted from one foot to the other, uncomfortable as Alex's predatory gaze washed over her.

"Ignore him," Maria said, shaking Ivy's hand. "You have to understand, we thought Jack was going to be a monk at the rate he was going. In fact, we were all so worried about him we planned on finding a woman for him at the campground this week. We're all relieved he already found someone on his own."

Ivy smiled. "I don't think you have to worry about Jack being a monk," she said. "That was his plan when he came to Shadow Lake, but I talked him out of it."

"How did you do that?" Alex asked.

"She smiled at me," Jack answered for Ivy, slipping his arm around her waist. "How was the traffic coming up here?"

"Not too bad," Alex replied. "It's not a holiday weekend, so that helped."

"Where do you live?" Ivy asked.

"We live in Bay City," Maria supplied. "Here, I'll make introductions since these two are such idiots. That couple over there arguing about if the trailer is level or not is Donnie Thompson and his girlfriend Lauren. They've been together about three years, and yet they're still not married. Most of us think Donnie is scared she'll say no, but we're going to work on him this week because if he's not careful, Lauren is going to take off on him because he's such a coward."

Ivy's eyes widened. "Um ... okay."

"That couple over there – the ones who look like they want to rip each other's hair out because the truck was backed in at an odd angle – is Scott and Melissa Graham," Maria said, pointing toward a brunette couple as they gestured angrily at one another. "They've been married for five years and they really do get along ... kind of. They had to drive up from Detroit, though, and it was a long five hours. They'll be fine once they eat and have a few beers."

"Good to know," Ivy said.

"I think you're overwhelming her," Jack chided.

"Oh, I don't mean to do that," Maria said, feigning innocence. "We should take a break from our gossip and focus on her. I'm just dying to hear about Miss Ivy and how she managed to snag you."

Ivy exchanged a worried look with Jack, a silent plea passing between them.

"You wanted to come camping, honey," Jack said, smirking. "Welcome to my world."

"SO, IVY, WHAT DO YOU DO FOR A LIVING?"

Jack's friends spent two hours setting up their campsites and then everyone grouped around the bonfire to eat dinner and gossip. Ivy was happy when the conversation involved old stories about Jack's wild college days, but when the onus was shifted to her she couldn't help but be uneasy.

"I own a plant nursery in Shadow Lake," Ivy replied, leaning back in her chair as Jack reached over and captured her hand.

"That's a cool job," Lauren said. "Did you go to school for that?"

"I didn't go to college," Ivy replied. "My father has always had an interest in plants and he taught me."

"You didn't go to college?" Maria furrowed her brow. "You missed out on the experience of a lifetime. Are you sad you didn't go?"

"Not really."

Jack squeezed Ivy's hand and fixed Maria with an unreadable look. "Ivy is very talented and she works really hard. College isn't everything, and she's done very well for herself."

"I didn't mean anything by it," Maria protested. "It's just ... don't you wish you would've been able to say you had an adventure?" She looked wistful.

"I have an adventure every day of my life when I go to work and stop my father from talking a customer's ear off," Ivy replied. "I'm not sure I was ever geared for college."

"How come?" Donnie asked, sipping his beer. "Is it because you have pink hair? You shouldn't worry about that. You would fit right in on a college campus with that hair."

Lauren smacked Donnie's knee. "Don't be rude."

"I didn't think I was being rude," Donnie offered ruefully. "I'm sorry."

"It's okay," Ivy said, wetting her lips and glancing down at her feet. "I just didn't ever want to go to college. I always knew I wanted to run a nursery. My dad helped me learn the things I needed to learn and gave me money to help with a down payment ... and then he just left me to do my thing."

"And you do it very well," Jack said, lifting their joined hands and pressing a kiss to Ivy's knuckles, earning exaggerated eye rolls from his male friends and soft sighs from the females.

"Do you make a lot of money?" Maria asked.

"Okay, that's enough of that," Jack said, straightening in his chair.

"It's okay, Jack," Ivy said. "They're curious because they thought you were going to be a monk for the rest of your life. I get it. To answer your question, yes, I make a nice living."

"Are you satisfied?" Jack asked, his eyes flashing.

"I honestly didn't mean anything by it, Jack," Maria said, holding her hands up. "She's just ... not what I expected. I thought when you finally found someone she would be more ... ."

"What?" Jack challenged.

"I was hoping she would be ugly so I could be the prettiest one in the group, if you must know," Maria replied. "Once I saw what she looked like naked – I'm so going on a diet, by the way – I was hoping she was stupid. Unfortunately, she's smart *and* pretty. Now I have to hate her."

Despite herself, Ivy chuckled as Jack relaxed back into his chair.

"She is definitely smart and pretty," Jack said.

"How did you two meet?" Melissa asked, changing the conversational topic to something less likely to set Jack off. "I'll bet it's a romantic story."

"I found a dead body in the ditch by my house and called the police," Ivy said. "That was Jack's first day on the job. When he met me I was barefoot and I yelled at him."

"And I was smitten from the first word that came out of her mouth," Jack added.

"Oh, nice," Alex said, nodding. "You had a dead body in your front yard, though? That had to suck."

"It wasn't fun," Ivy said.

"Did you start dating right away?" Lauren asked.

"No," Ivy answered. "In fact, Jack made sure I knew in no uncertain terms that he did not come to Shadow Lake to date. He told me about eight times the first week we met."

"That's insulting," Maria said, making a face. "You don't say that to a woman out of the blue like that. How did you know she even liked you?"

"I could tell she liked me by the way she undressed me with her eyes whenever we were alone," Jack replied, laughing when Ivy shot him a murderous look. "What? Are you going to sit there and deny you thought I was hot the day we met?"

"I didn't think you were hot," Ivy argued. "I thought you were interesting to look at. I wouldn't take that as a compliment. I find Pee-wee Herman interesting to look at too."

Jack's friends broke into uproarious laughter as his smile tipped down. "Are you honestly saying you weren't attracted to me right away?"

"Actually, the second I saw you I thought you were very attractive," Ivy conceded. "I also thought you were a pain in the ass because you kept telling me I was imagining the body in the ditch."

"That is not my fault," Jack shot back. "You were wandering around the middle of the road in a skirt and no shoes. I thought there was a distinct possibility you were crazy."

"Was I right about the body?"

Jack's nostril's flared as he gripped the arms of his chair. "It's been great catching up," he said after a moment. "It's getting late, though, and Ivy and I need to go to bed."

Ivy raised her eyebrows. She knew exactly what that was code for. Fighting with her – no matter how minor the argument – turned Jack on. "I am really tired."

"Of course you are," Jack said, helping her up from her chair. "We had a really long day."

"When we got here you two were sleeping after having sex," Scott argued. "How long could your day have possibly been?"

"Are you blind?" Melissa asked, slapping his arm. "That's what they're going to do now. They're not really tired. That argument flipped Jack's switch."

"How could you possibly see that from across the fire?"

"It's obvious whenever they look at each other," Maria said, smirking as Jack supplied everyone with a tight smile and a half-hearted wave.

"We'll see everyone for breakfast," Jack said, pushing Ivy toward their tent. "Do not come over there to wake us up. We'll wake up on our own."

"Have fun," Alex called to their retreating backs, laughing when he heard Ivy squeal as Jack caught up with her. "What do you make of that?"

"He's happy," Lauren said. "That makes me happy for him because I wasn't sure he would ever be happy again after what happened with his partner."

"I'm happy for him, too," Melissa said. "I wish he would let us get to know Ivy better, but I'm sure that will happen when he relaxes a little bit. He's like a pit bull where she's concerned."

"I think he's in love," Donnie said, shaking his head when he heard Ivy's laughter roll in their direction from the darkness.

"He barely knows her," Maria scoffed.

"I don't think that matters," Scott said. "He can't take his eyes off of her, and she seems equally taken with him."

"That's just lust," Maria argued.

"I think it's more than that," Scott said. "We'll know more tomorrow. They were both a little tense tonight."

"I've got twenty bucks that says Jack marries her before six months pass – or at least proposes," Donnie said.

"I'll take that bet," Alex said. "I think it's going to be three months."

"I'll take that bet, too," Maria said. "I think you're both crazy, though. Ivy Morgan is just a fad. Jack will spend three months sleeping with her and then move on."

"Oh, that shows how much women know," Donnie scoffed. "Jack Harker is already off the market. He's a goner … and after seeing that woman naked, I can totally see why."

"You're a pig," Lauren muttered.

"And proud of it."

The six friends chatted long into the night, no one worried about going to bed early. In the nearby tent, Jack and Ivy did what came naturally: gazed at the stars … and then fought so they could make up.

Five

"Where did you learn to cook like that, Ivy," Donnie asked the next morning, scraping his plastic fork against his plate to make sure he ate every morsel available. "That was the best omelet I've ever had."

"That was pretty impressive," Maria said. "Now I have to hate you because you can cook, too. Is there anything you can't do?"

"Lose an argument," Jack supplied, tickling Ivy's ribs when she shot him a dark look.

"I learned to cook around a fire from my mother," Ivy explained. "We used to go camping a lot when I was a kid."

"Did you come here?" Lauren asked.

"A few times."

"Until the dogman scared you away," Jack teased, instantly wishing he could yank the words back into his mouth when he saw the look on Ivy's face. Her anger wasn't feigned this time.

"What's the dogman?" Alex asked.

"Nothing," Jack answered swiftly. "It's a private joke. We were … playing a game yesterday."

"I saw what game you were playing," Donnie said. "It looked fun. Tell us the joke."

"We all saw what game they were playing and there's no reason to talk about it again," Melissa countered. "In fact, let's talk about what we're going to do today."

"I don't want to do anything but relax," Maria volunteered. "No offense to everyone else, but this is the first day of vacation and I'm determined to get a tan. All I want to do is hang out here with a book and a beer."

"That sounds good to me," Melissa said.

"Me, too," Lauren chimed in.

"Well, I want to look around," Scott said. "We came here last year and I remember it having a lot of good hiking paths. Does anyone else want to go on a hike?"

"That sounds good to me," Alex said. "Do you want to come with us, Ivy? You're the only one who knows this area really well. Maybe you can show us something we missed."

"I would love to," Ivy said. "Just let me put some different shoes on."

"You can stay with us if you want, Ivy," Maria offered. "We won't bite … and we would love to grill you about Jack and what he's been up to over the past few months."

"She's coming with us," Jack said, pushing himself to his feet. "I don't trust you guys not to peck her to death while I'm gone."

"Ivy looks like she can handle herself," Lauren pointed out. "If she can handle you, she can handle anything."

Jack shrugged. "Maybe I want to spend the morning handling her in the woods. Did you ever consider that?"

"Right on," Donnie said.

"Men are pigs," Lauren muttered.

"ARE YOU DOING OKAY?" JACK ASKED TWENTY MINUTES LATER, watching as Ivy climbed over a fallen log.

"I'm fine, Jack," Ivy said. "You don't have to worry about me. I like your friends."

"To be fair, they're not all my friends," Jack clarified. "I lived with

Donnie, Scott, and Alex in college, but the women are more recent additions."

"Like me."

"No one is like you, honey," Jack said following her around a large pine tree as she scanned the ground. "That's why I like you ... although ... what are you doing?"

"Looking for bear tracks," Ivy replied, not missing a beat. "Do you see that mark there?" She pointed to the tree trunk where a section of bark was missing.

Jack nodded.

"A bear did that."

Jack glanced around, suddenly nervous. "Are you messing with me because of that whole dogman thing? If you are, I deserve it and I'm sorry. It kind of slipped out."

"I'm not happy with that because your friends already think I'm a bohemian freak, but that's really a bear mark," Ivy said. "Max taught me when we were in middle school. He was obsessed with being a bear tracker for like two years."

Jack snorted, although he was still nervous. "A bear won't eat me, right?"

"A bear will not eat you," Ivy confirmed. "There aren't a lot of bears in this area. The ones that are around will be scared by noise, so they won't go too close to camp as long as people don't leave food scattered around where they can get at it."

"I wasn't scared," Jack offered, squaring his shoulders. "I just wanted to know if any were around in case I needed to protect you."

"Duly noted," Ivy said, patting his chest. "Don't worry. If a bear comes around I'll make sure you're safe."

"You're a pain in the butt," Jack muttered, grabbing her around the waist and twirling her off the ground. "I'm glad you're here, though."

"I'm glad I'm here, too," Ivy said, laughing when Jack kissed the tip of her nose and placed her back on the ground.

"If you don't like those women, I understand," Jack said, keeping his voice low. "I'm not sure how fond I am of any of them. I like the guys, though, and I don't want to alienate them."

"Jack, I know what those women see when they look at me," Ivy said. "It's okay. It's not like we're going to be best friends, but everyone is getting along. You don't have to worry about them grilling me either. I'm fine with it. They're curious because of you, not me."

"Don't kid yourself, Ivy," Jack countered. "They might be curious because you're dating me, but I can guarantee they've never met anyone like you – and it's not just because you're one of a kind. They're dying to get to know more about you."

"We're *all* dying to get to know more about Ivy," Alex said, appearing from the other side of the tree. "You know your voices carry in the woods, right?"

Ivy's cheeks burned as Alex's pointed gaze bounced between Jack and her. "I ... ."

"Don't worry about it," Alex said, waving off whatever lame apology Ivy was about to utter. "I understand that you might be a little uncomfortable regarding what happened last night. We don't want you feeling like an outsider, though."

"She's not an outsider," Jack said, reaching for Ivy's hand. "She's with me ... and she's going to stay with me for a really long time."

"You are just too cute for words," Alex said, mock clutching the spot over his heart. "I haven't seen you this worked up over a woman since sophomore year of college. Do you remember Sydney Armstrong?"

Jack frowned as Ivy tried to rein in her laughter.

"I don't want to talk about that," Jack said.

"I want to talk about it," Ivy said, shifting excitedly from one foot to the other. "I'm dying to hear about Jack's old girlfriend."

"She wasn't Jack's girlfriend," Alex supplied. "He just wanted her to be his girlfriend."

"Well, now I definitely want to know," Ivy said, grinning.

"We don't talk about your ex-boyfriends," Jack argued. "Why do we have to talk about my ... old crush?"

"You met the only ex-boyfriend of note I have," Ivy reminded him. "He started a cult so he could sleep with women and steal their money while his protégé stalked and tried to kill me. Did you forget that?"

"I could never forget that," Jack said, his heart rolling at the memory. He'd been convinced he was going to lose Ivy that night –

even though he wasn't certain he wanted her in the way she deserved at the time – and every step through the dark woods by her house was one filled with fear and dread. "My story pales in comparison to your story."

"Your ex-boyfriend started a cult?" Alex asked, impressed.

"It's not as cool as it sounds," Ivy said. "Besides, he's in prison now for scamming people out of money. His cult is ... no more."

"And I had to eat mushrooms that tasted like feet because of that guy," Jack added.

"How does that work?" Alex was intrigued by the story.

"Well, we were spying on the cult and we got caught," Jack said. "Ivy lied and said we were hunting for mushrooms ... something called morels that are only out in the spring ... and then she actually made me hunt for mushrooms."

"Those mushrooms are a delicacy," Ivy sniffed.

"They tasted like dirty underwear, honey."

Alex chuckled. "You guys are a trip," he said. "I like how comfortable you are together. I don't remember the last time I saw Jack this relaxed. Well, I do, but ... ." Alex trailed off, thinking better of bringing up Jack's ordeal.

"Ivy knows what happened to me," Jack said, rubbing the back of her neck. "We've talked all about it. She knows I was shot and how it happened."

"You're a brave woman for taking him on," Alex said, going for jocularity instead of somber reflection. "I already like that he's done nothing but smile since he introduced you to us."

"I like that she was naked when we first saw her," Donnie said, moving in from the left with Scott at his heels. "These woods are thick. I'm afraid we're going to get lost and die of starvation."

Ivy rolled her eyes. "The lake is a quarter of a mile that way," she said, pointing to her right. "If you walk to it you can follow the shoreline back to camp. It's not a very big lake."

Donnie was sheepish. "It's not fair that you know things like that," he said. "The only thing Lauren knows how to do is pick nail polish."

The men laughed while Ivy tamped down her irritation.

"I'm sure she knows more than that," Ivy said.

"It was a joke," Donnie said, moving in the direction of the lake. "Let's go this way. I don't want to run the risk of Ivy deciding she hates me and purposely ditching me in the woods."

"You don't have to worry about that," Ivy offered. "If I was going to kill you I would tie a hotdog around your neck and let the bears get you."

Jack couldn't help but laugh as a worried look flitted across Donnie's face. "And that's why I try to stay on her good side," he said, hurrying to catch up with Ivy as she trudged toward the lake.

"She is terrifying," Donnie said, falling into step behind the couple. "That makes her really hot. You know that, right?"

"Everything she does makes her really hot," Jack said.

"Including fighting?" Scott teased. "You seemed to like it when she argued with you last night."

"I'm not going to lie, the fighting turns me on," Jack admitted, earning a sidelong look from Ivy. "I like her heart and giving spirit the best, though."

"Oh, so sweet," Donnie cooed, earning snickers from his friends. "You guys should be in a romance novel."

"I can live with that," Jack said, glancing down and smiling when Ivy slipped her hand into his.

"I have no idea how this happened, but you're somehow a romantic at heart," Alex mused, watching with interest as Ivy easily stepped around an indentation in the ground that he would've missed if it wasn't for her. "So she's hot, she's smart, she cooks, and she knows her way around the woods. Seriously, she's like the perfect woman."

"I agree," Jack said. "She's mine, though. Don't get any ideas."

"You don't have a sister, do you, Ivy?" Donnie asked. "They should clone you."

"I have a brother," Ivy replied. "I don't think he's your type. He thinks he got all the looks in our family, though, so if you're really desperate ... ."

"I'm never going to be that desperate," Donnie said. "Still ... do you think he'd wear a dress? Just in case, I mean."

This time everyone broke into enthusiastic guffaws, including Jack and Ivy. Ivy was so caught up in everyone's laughter – and the merriment of the afternoon – she almost ignored the niggling warning at the back of her mind.

She released Jack's hand and took a step away from him, focusing on the area to her left. Alex, Donnie, and Scott didn't immediately notice when she broke off from the group, but Jack followed her.

"What is it?" he murmured, keeping his voice low.

"I don't know," Ivy admitted. "I … something is over here. I'm almost sure of it."

Jack glanced over his shoulder at his friends. They seemed oblivious to Ivy and Jack's conversation. "How important do you think it is to go and look over there?"

"I don't know."

"Well, let's check it out," Jack said.

Ivy shifted her eyes to Jack's, momentarily worried. "You should go with your friends," she suggested. "I can catch up in a few minutes. It's probably nothing. In fact, it's probably my imagination."

"Or perhaps it's something and we both should go together," Jack countered. "I'm not letting you go alone. We've been through too much – seen too many strange things – to risk anything of the sort. We're going together."

"What are you going to tell your friends?"

Jack's smile was impish. "You're probably not going to like this, but it's the one thing that I know will work," he said, pressing a quick kiss to her forehead before turning to the others. "Um, guys, do you mind walking back alone? Ivy and I want to take a nature walk just the two of us."

"Are you guys animals or something?" Donnie challenged.

"We just like to play them when we're in the woods," Jack replied, his tone easy and disarming. "The lake is right over there. You can follow it back to camp. We shouldn't be too long."

"I wouldn't brag about that," Scott teased. "We'll be fine. You two have fun."

"We definitely will."

Six

Jack kept one ear on their surroundings as he followed Ivy farther into the woods, refusing to let her out of his sight no matter how capable she appeared.

"Don't get too far ahead of me," Jack ordered, snagging the back of Ivy's shirt and pulling her back when he got caught up on a tree branch. "I will not be happy if I get lost out here, honey."

"I think you're worried I'm about to get us into trouble," Ivy countered, patiently waiting for Jack to right himself.

"I've learned not to second-guess your intuition," Jack said, his expression serious. "I don't know exactly what's going on with you, but in case you've forgotten, you saved my life a couple of weeks ago. I have faith you know what you're doing."

"I haven't forgotten," Ivy said. "I plan on lording it over you in exchange for sexual favors for months to come."

"I'll gladly put up with it," Jack said, falling into step next to her and remaining alert. "What did you ... feel?"

"I don't know," Ivy hedged. "It's probably nothing."

"You obviously don't feel that it's nothing, otherwise you wouldn't have stopped," Jack prodded. "I saw the look on your face. If I didn't know better, I would've thought you were hearing something."

"Did anyone else notice?" Ivy was worried Jack's friends would realize she was even more different than they already ascertained. "Maybe I should go home so you don't have to explain any of this."

"Shut your mouth," Jack said, rolling his eyes.

"Don't tell me to shut my mouth!"

"When you say something stupid, I'm going to tell you to shut your mouth," Jack shot back. "I want you with me."

"What if they decide they don't like me and want you to break up with me?"

"Hey, they already like you," Jack said. "You're making a lot of this stuff up in your head."

"Those women don't like me," Ivy argued. "They think I belong at some beatnik coffee shop serving drinks and going to raves every weekend."

It was a serious conversation, but Jack couldn't stop himself from chuckling. "Ivy, you're usually the last person who cares about what others think of you. Why is this bugging you now?"

"They're your oldest friends."

"That doesn't mean I care what they think," Jack said. "I'm friendly with Donnie, Alex, and Scott because we went to college together. We don't have a lot in common now, and it's not like we're best buds or anything.

"We talk every few months and email off-color jokes to one another, but that's pretty much the end of it," he continued. "This camping trip was a way for them to reach out to me because I wasn't exactly chomping at the bit to hang out with people after I was shot."

"So you don't care if they despise me?" Ivy wasn't convinced Jack's friends couldn't sway his decision, and she hated herself for the bout of insecurity.

"No," Jack replied, not missing a beat. "I only care if I like you, and I think we've determined that I can't stay away from you. Ivy, I'm sorry if I did you a disservice by not inviting you camping right away. That was not my intent. I was worried you were going to turn me down. It had nothing to do with you."

"I don't want you to apologize," Ivy said, shaking her head. "I'm sorry I'm being so neurotic. I guess ... I can't help it. Part of me is worried that you'll walk away and I can't seem to shake it."

"That's on me," Jack said, brushing her hair away from her face. "I got so worked up after you were shot that I shut down. That's not your fault."

"I understand why you did it," Ivy said. "You panicked about your own shooting and got overwhelmed. It's not fair to keep punishing you for it when I've already forgiven you."

"You have a right to feel what you feel," Jack countered. "I deserve whatever you throw at me. I am really sorry, though, and I have no intention of going anywhere. I like you because you're you. Nothing is going to change that."

"Even if I lead us to something awful?" Ivy asked, lifting her eyes.

"Even if you lead me to something awful," Jack confirmed. "Do you want to know why?"

Ivy nodded.

"Because I found something wonderful here," he said, tapping the spot above her heart. "You and I are muddling through this the best we can. It's all going to work out in the end. I believe that. I think you should, too."

"I believe in you," Ivy said, leaning in for a quick hug. "Now I just need to figure out what's bugging me out here."

"Let's hope it's nothing worse than the dogman," Jack said, pressing a quick kiss to Ivy's forehead before releasing her. "Bigfoot I can handle. I'm manly. Trust me."

"You're ... something," Ivy said, although her eyes twinkled as she returned to their trek. "I wish I knew what was bugging me. It was like I had a feeling that something was watching me."

"Like the day you were gardening and you thought I was watching you?"

"I ... don't know," Ivy said. "I felt something that day. I didn't jump to the conclusion that it was you until I saw you down by the lake. Before then ... I was uncomfortable."

"And you didn't tell me you thought someone was watching you," Jack grumbled.

"I was very angry with you that day."

"And rightfully so," Jack said. "I don't want to fight about that again ... at least until we're alone and can make up properly. Follow your instincts, Ivy. What do you feel?"

"There's something over here," Ivy said, pointing. "I have no idea what it is."

"Well, let's see what it is," Jack said, grabbing her hand and moving ahead of her so he would be the first one in harm's way should they come across trouble. "You be ready to run if I tell you to do it."

"I'm not leaving you."

"If there's danger, you are leaving me," Jack challenged.

"I didn't leave you at the house when your ex-partner's murderous spirit was trying to kill you, and I'm not leaving you now."

"You are the most stubborn person I've ever met," Jack muttered, pushing through the trees and walking into a small clearing in the middle of the forest. "Is this where we're supposed to be?"

Ivy tilted her head to the side, considering. "Yes."

"Well, I don't see anything here, but let's look around," Jack instructed. "Don't you leave me. Do you understand?"

"Is that because you're worried about me or getting lost?"

"Both," Jack replied, squeezing her hand before releasing it. "If you feel anything ... ."

"I'll scream like a girl and jump into your arms so you can protect me," Ivy finished, making a face.

"That sounds delightful," Jack said, refusing to let an argument fester. "Maybe we'll play that game in our tent tonight."

"You're a sick man."

"I do my best," Jack said, his eyes moving around the clearing. He was already on the job, even though he had no idea what he was supposed to be looking for. The clearing wasn't very large, and nothing stood out to Jack's trained eye. He decided to approach things as an investigator, and moved along the tree line, completely circling it and then moving in closer to make sure he didn't miss anything.

For her part, Ivy was drawn to a large rock in the center of the clearing. Something about it called to her, although she had no idea what. An indentation caught her attention near the base of the rock, the soft dirt there upturned and showing off a rather large paw print.

Jack moved to Ivy's side when he saw her kneel. "What are you looking at?"

"I'm not sure," Ivy answered. "It looks like an animal print."

"What kind of animal? If it's a bear, we're out of here. I'm manly, but I can't take on a bear."

"You just told me that you could take on the dogman," Ivy reminded him. "A bear should be nothing compared to the dogman."

"Yes, but if I tell you I can take on Santa Claus, that doesn't mean I can take on all men in red suits, does it?" Jack countered. "The dogman isn't real."

"You don't know that," Ivy challenged.

"Are you saying you believe in Bigfoot?" Jack cocked a dubious eyebrow.

"I'm saying that there are a lot of things out there we don't know about," Ivy clarified. "I didn't believe in dream walking before we did it either."

"You have a point," Jack said, sighing.

For months – including long before they declared themselves a couple – Jack and Ivy shared nightly interludes in their sleep. Neither one of them mentioned it, initially believing they were the only ones having the dreams. Once they realized they were actually experiencing the dreams together, things took an interesting turn.

While Jack's dreams were plagued with memories of his former partner shooting him and leaving him for dead on a Detroit street, Ivy's appearance eased that problem and he rarely revisited that particular nightmare. Ivy could control their destinations, and she preferred sandy beaches and fruity cocktails to grim and dirty urban settings.

They didn't dream walk every night, even though that was the case in the beginning. Jack was convinced their subconscious minds didn't need to cling to each other in sleep because their physical bodies were together in the same bed every night. He still enjoyed their dream manifestations, but sometimes it was nice to know he was alone when his mind worked out the events of the day.

"You've also seen a spirit jump from one body to another – and manage to control it," Ivy reminded him. "I'm pretty sure you didn't think that was possible either."

"I get it, Ivy," Jack said. "I didn't mean to cast aspersions on Bigfoot. It's just … that's one of those things you see on television and discard because it's so surreal."

"I'm not saying I believe in Bigfoot, Jack," Ivy said, dusting her hands off on her knees as she straightened. "I'm just saying that's not a bear track."

"Okay, I'll play. What do you think it is?" Jack asked.

Ivy shrugged. She didn't have an answer.

"Could it be a wolf?" Jack pressed, leaning over so he could get a look at the print. "It's big, don't get me wrong, but it still looks like a dog print to me."

"That's about twice the size of a dog print," Ivy said. "I guess it's not out of the realm of possibility that it's a wolf. They have reintroduced some in the Upper Peninsula. I've never heard of one around here, though."

"What about a coyote?"

"A coyote is smaller," Ivy replied. "They're also scavengers. They're more likely to go through your garbage – or grab your poodle from the yard – than hang out in this area."

"You just want it to be the dogman," Jack said, his face splitting into a grin. "Admit it."

"From a purely scientific approach, I would love to see the dogman," Ivy confirmed. "I don't really believe in the dogman, though. Although … I don't know. Maybe I believe in the dogman. I honestly have no idea."

"I love how cute you are when you get scientific," Jack said, slinging an arm over Ivy's shoulders and pulling her close. "I don't know what to tell you, honey. Other than this print – and I'm not sure what we're really looking at here – there's nothing in this clearing. Are you sure this is where we were supposed to come?"

"Whatever I was feeling earlier is gone," Ivy said. "You're right. It's just an open space in the middle of the woods. I'm sorry for dragging you away from your friends."

"I'm not," Jack said. "I like spending time with you. Even if nothing is here, I'm glad we had a few minutes alone together. It's okay. I'm kind of relieved there's nothing here."

"I guess," Ivy said, her eyes distant as they scanned the trees one more time. "I don't understand why I felt the need to come here. It feels stupid now."

"Don't let it bother you, honey," Jack said, leading her back in the direction of the camp. "Nothing was lost, and at least now you won't dwell on it. Let's go back to camp and take a nap before dinner."

Ivy snorted. "Everyone is sitting around camp," she reminded him. "They'll know what we're doing."

"I don't care."

"What if I care?"

"I'll talk you out of caring," Jack said, urging Ivy forward with his hand at the small of her back as they exited the clearing. "I have powers of persuasion that will boggle your mind."

"I already know that," Ivy said.

Jack was almost beyond the tree line when he paused, the hair on the back of his neck standing at attention. He turned swiftly, expecting to find another camper – or even one of his friends back for another round of teasing. The small expanse remained empty, though.

"What's wrong?" Ivy asked, instantly on alert.

"Nothing," Jack said, shaking his head and forcing a smile. "Now I'm convinced the dogman is out there and I was just checking to make sure he didn't follow us."

"I'm not napping with you if you keep making fun of me."

"And we're done talking about the dogman," Jack teased, tickling Ivy's ribs as he cast a final glance over his shoulder. They were alone. He was sure of it.

So why did he feel like someone was watching them?

Seven

"Where are you guys going?" Maria asked twenty minutes later, her gaze zeroing in on Ivy and Jack as they moved toward their tent.

"We're going to take a nap," Jack replied, not caring in the least that everyone knew sleeping was the furthest thing from his mind.

"Didn't you just do that in the woods?" Donnie asked. He sat next to the campfire with Alex and Scott, his expression full of mirth and teasing. "Seriously, are you animals or something?"

"We didn't nap in the woods," Jack replied. "We took a walk."

"I think you did more than walk."

"Hey, I am not risking getting Poison Ivy in a dangerous place," Jack shot back, gesturing toward his groin. "Trust me. That will never happen to me."

Ivy snorted, her mind going back to an incident shortly after she met Jack. "That's right," she said. "Jack knows all about Poison Ivy."

"Do tell," Alex prodded.

"He just fell in some accidentally one day," Ivy replied, pressing her lips together to keep from laughing.

"I still maintain you knew that Poison Ivy was there and wanted me to fall into it," Jack charged. "That was the first time you saw me with my shirt off. I believe there was actual drool on the floor when you got finished rubbing lotion all over me."

"Nice," Donnie said, pumping his fist. "These are the stories I want to hear."

"You're so full of yourself," Ivy scoffed. "You cried like a baby when that happened. I'm the one who had to warn you not to put your hands in your pants, otherwise you would've really found yourself in a world of hurt."

"Oh, that's priceless," Alex said, barking out a hoarse laugh. "Poison Ivy brought you and Ivy together, Jack. That's almost poetic … even if you did cry."

"I did not cry," Jack snapped.

"You wanted to," Ivy interjected.

Jack grabbed her around the waist and pushed her toward their tent. "I'm going to make you cry," he muttered.

"You just want me to check your pants to make sure there's no Poison Ivy."

"That's a very good suggestion, honey." Jack looked over at his friends. "We'll be back in twenty minutes … thirty tops. We won't be long."

"You need to stop bragging about stuff like that," Alex said.

"JACK, CAN YOU BRING ME THAT LONG CONTAINER FROM THE cooler?" Ivy asked a half hour later, relaxed and refreshed after a nice … nap. "It's the flat one on top."

Jack retrieved the item in question and delivered it to Ivy, dropping a kiss on the back of her head as he watched her work. "What are you making us for lunch?"

"Quesadillas."

Maria glanced over from the peanut butter and jelly sandwiches she was slapping together. "Seriously? You're making him quesadillas?"

Ivy stilled. "Um … ."

"Don't let her get to you," Jack chided. "Quesadillas sound great. Don't bother my woman, Maria. She's a master in the kitchen."

"You said she made you eat mushrooms that tasted like feet,"

Donnie challenged from his spot next to the bonfire. "That doesn't sound like she's a master in the kitchen."

"I'll have you know that the rest of that pasta dish tasted like Heaven in a bowl," Jack replied. "Only the mushrooms were bad."

"You don't have to worry about me making you anything with morels again, Jack," Ivy said. "When spring comes back around, Max and I will disappear in the woods to find mushrooms and you can eat fast food for those two weeks."

"I can live with that," Jack said, moving to sit on the bench so he could watch Ivy work. He was fascinated by her kitchen prowess – even more than usual now that they were out in the open and didn't have an oven to work with. "If you and Max get lost in the woods, though, don't come crying to me to find you."

"Do you think Max and I get lost in the woods often?" Ivy asked, sprinkling cheese on two tortilla shells.

"I'm surprised Max can find his way out of bed every morning," Jack shot back.

"Who is Max?" Lauren asked, doling lunchmeat onto bread across the table from Ivy.

"He's my brother," Ivy answered. "He and Jack like to compete so they can see who is more macho."

"I've already won that competition," Jack said, knitting his eyebrows together as he watched Ivy slip slices of onion, red peppers, and tomato into the quesadilla. "That looks good."

"I'm not done with yours yet," Ivy said, grabbing a baggie full of chopped chicken breast from the corner of the Tupperware bin and dropping it into his quesadilla before adding more cheese and gently placing another tortilla shell on top of it. "We can only cook one at a time, so I'll do yours first."

"I can do it," Jack offered. "You just put them all together."

"I want to do it for you."

Jack narrowed his eyes. "You think I'm going to ruin it, don't you?"

"I think you're extremely handsome and I want to cook it for you so I don't spend the entire afternoon drooling over you," Ivy replied.

"It's a good thing you're cute, because I'm not sure if I could put up with that mouth otherwise," Jack said, giving her a soft kiss. "I'm going to join the men by the fire if you have no further need of my assistance."

"I'm good until after lunch. Then I might need another nap."

"Cute, cute, cute," Jack said, sliding off the bench so he could join Alex, Scott, and Donnie at the center of the campsite. Jack watched Ivy carry the cast iron skillet to the other side of the fire and arrange two logs until she had them exactly how she wanted them. The determined tilt of her chin caused him to smile ... and then he realized the other three men were staring at him. "What?"

"You're so ... funny ... with her," Donnie said. "You can't take your eyes off of her."

"She's pretty," Jack said, winking at Ivy.

"She's definitely pretty," Alex agreed. "You're happy, though."

"She's funny, too," Jack said.

"Personally, I think you're a little whipped," Donnie offered. "I'm sure you'll outgrow that eventually." He frowned down at his lap when Lauren unceremoniously dropped a paper plate with a sandwich on it on top of his thighs and then added a bag of potato chips to the growing pile. "Of course, you're getting a quesadilla and I'm getting tuna fish. I think there's a lesson in that."

"I think there's a lesson in that, too," Jack said. "And, for the record, I'm fine being whipped. You should see what she can do with pasta."

"ARE YOU COLD?" JACK ASKED, SETTLING IVY ON HIS LAP shortly after sunset and wrapping a blanket around both of them so they could get comfortable. The day was warm, but as soon as the sun slipped below the horizon a chill settled in the air.

"I'm good," Ivy said, snuggling closer to Jack so she could rest her head against his shoulder. "I like nights like this. We should build a fire pit behind my house so we can do this at home."

"We can do that," Jack said. "I've seen those bin things you're supposed to use to ring the pit after you dig into the ground at Max's lumberyard. I can get one there."

"And Max can help you," Ivy offered. "That sounds like a great way for you guys to flex and compete for an entire afternoon."

"This Max sounds funny," Alex said. "Is he older or younger than you?"

"Older," Ivy replied. "Despite his competition with Jack, we're actually pretty close."

"But you hate him, right, Jack?" Alex pressed.

"I like Max a great deal," Jack answered. "I find him to be completely annoying a lot of the time, but he's dedicated to Ivy and he goes all out to protect her."

"Why would he need to protect her?"

"Um ... ." Jack scanned Ivy's face, choosing his words carefully. "I told you about the body in the ditch when we first met, right?"

Everyone nodded.

"The man who killed that woman and left her in Ivy's yard ended up going after Ivy," Jack explained. "Max thought I was a prowler one day and jumped me."

Scott barked out a laugh. "Is he still alive?"

"I didn't know who he was, but when I realized what was going on I was glad Ivy had protection," Jack replied. "To be fair, this was long before we started dating. I was still trying to figure her out – and why I couldn't stop thinking about her."

"That sounds freaky," Melissa said. "How did the guy end up getting caught?"

"He chased me through the woods by my house and then Jack swooped in to rescue me at the last minute," Ivy answered. "He was my hero."

"Somehow I think you would've found a way out of that situation without me," Jack said, squeezing Ivy's waist beneath the blanket. "I'm glad I was there, though."

"Is that when you first kissed?" Lauren asked, a dreamy expression on her face.

"Believe it or not, our first kiss came after the Poison Ivy fiasco," Jack said, smirking at the memory. "I told you she drooled when she saw me without my shirt on. She did a little more than that, too."

"Oh, something tells me she didn't do that alone," Maria scoffed. "Did you guys start dating right away after you saved her?"

"Nope," Jack said. "I remained an idiot for another two weeks or so. Then I gave in. I couldn't go another day without her."

"Oh, that's so romantic," Lauren sighed. "How come you never say romantic things like that about me?" She poked Donnie's side. "Jack can't stop saying romantic things about Ivy."

"I ... ." Donnie didn't have an answer. "Thanks a lot, Jack. You're making me look bad."

Jack shrugged and rested his chin on Ivy's shoulder. "That's your problem."

"Does anyone know any ghost stories?" Maria asked, popping the tab on a beer. "We're sitting around a bonfire. I love ghost stories."

"That sounds fun," Lauren interjected. "I love ghost stories, too."

"I only know romance novel stories," Melissa said. "How about you, Ivy? You camped a lot when you were younger. You must know some ghost stories."

"Ivy only knows dogman stories," Jack teased, practically daring her to make a scene regarding the good-natured ribbing.

"What's the dogman?" Alex asked, intrigued. "Is that like a werewolf?"

"It's Bigfoot," Jack replied, keeping a firm grip on Ivy in case she tried to wriggle off his lap. "Ivy was afraid of him when she was younger because people at this campground told her he was real."

"No more naps for you," Ivy muttered.

Jack tugged on his limited patience and brushed her hair away from her face. "You were a kid," he said. "There's nothing to be embarrassed about. Now I know what I'm going to dress up as for Halloween, though."

"Oh, no, you're going to dress up like a schmuck," Ivy said. "Then you're not even going to have to buy a costume."

Jack kissed her cheek, refusing to embrace the potential argument. "Tell them a dogman story," he cajoled. "Please?"

"Tell us one," Maria pressed. "I love this idea. I didn't know there were Bigfoot sightings in this area. Now I want to find him."

Ivy stilled, surprised. "You believe in Bigfoot?"

"I would love to believe in Bigfoot," Maria replied. "I'm not sure I really do, but the idea of Bigfoot is fun. I grew up in Detroit. We didn't have Bigfoot. My mom did warn me about the guy who dressed like a clown on the corner by the pharmacy who kept asking me to see if I could find his rubber nose in his pocket."

"Oh, gross," Ivy said, making a face.

"Just for the record, he's not called Bigfoot here," Jack said. "He's called the dogman."

"You're like a fountain of useless information, man," Alex deadpanned.

Jack rolled his eyes. "Tell them one story, Ivy," he prodded. "I'll reward you with a massage later if you do."

"You're going to be massaging me for the rest of your life at this point," Ivy shot back.

"That's a job I will happily take on," Jack said. "Come on. Just one."

"This is secondhand," Ivy warned, reluctantly relaxing into Jack's embrace. "I was a kid when I heard the story. Then my brother jumped out of some bushes with mud caked all over his face and tree branches sticking out of his hair and scared the bejeezus out of me."

"I told you I would beat him up next time I saw him," Jack said. "Come on."

"Okay, the lady who told the story was named Nancy Bristow," Ivy said, launching into her tale. "She claims she was outside putting feed in her birdhouse one day and she heard a noise. They lived out by the Jordan River Valley, and that's the area where a lot of the dogman tales originate.

"Anyway, at first she thought it was an animal — maybe a raccoon or something — but after a few more noises she realized it was too big for that," she continued. "Then she thought it might be a deer because they came into her yard and ate from the birdfeeder.

"When she looked over her shoulder, she swears up and down she saw a tall animal on two legs," Ivy said. "It had a long snout like a wolf and it was looking at her. She freaked out and ran into the house."

"That's not so scary," Alex scoffed.

"The next morning she turned on the television and saw that the neighbor two doors down had gone missing," Ivy said. "Actually, it was his teenage daughter. They assumed she was out doing teenager things, but when she didn't return home later that day they sent out a search party."

"Did they ever find her?" Jack asked.

"They found what was left of her shortly before sunset," Ivy replied. "Her body was about a mile behind Nancy's house and she'd been torn apart, with some of her … flesh … eaten. They couldn't match the dental imprints to any known predators in the area – canine or otherwise – and supposedly the case is still open."

"Holy crap," Maria said, glancing over her shoulder to scan the dark woods. "Did Nancy ever see the dogman again?"

"She claims that she was hiking by Dead Man's Hill one day and caught movement out of the corner of her eye," Ivy responded. "When she glanced over, she swears she saw the same creature that was watching her from the woods that day. He was walking in the woods – kind of keeping pace with her – and she freaked out and ran back to her car."

"Omigod!" Lauren said, clutching Donnie's hand. "How far is Dead Man's Hill from here?"

"Like a half hour away," Ivy said.

"Did you ever see the dogman?" Scott asked.

"Just when my brother pretended to be him."

"Okay, I'm officially freaked out," Maria admitted.

"And I'm officially turned on," Jack whispered. "That was a marvelous story, honey. I'm going to rub you until you beg me to stop."

"Promises, promises," Ivy scoffed.

"Just you wait," Jack said. "I'm going to make that story worth your while … and then some."

Eight

"We're going to spend the afternoon in town today," Jack announced the next morning, his fingers linked with Ivy's as they strolled toward his truck.

Maria, bleary-eyed from all the beer she drank the night before, fixed the couple with a disdainful look. "Why?"

"Because we want to go to some museum Ivy told me about and have lunch at her favorite Mexican restaurant," Jack replied, nonplussed. "You look rough, by the way. How is that hangover?"

"I blame it on the dogman story," Maria intoned, rubbing her forehead. "I was too freaked out to sleep, so I had to drink until I could pass out."

"If that's your story," Jack said, chuckling.

"How can you two be so chipper this early in the morning?" Donnie asked, rubbing his neck with one hand as he poked at the fire to get it going with the other. "It's inhuman."

"If you recall, Ivy and I turned in hours before the rest of you," Jack replied. "We did not get drunk, so we don't have hangovers."

"No, you two have sex hangovers," Alex said, reaching for a bottle of water. "That's better than this type of hangover, let me tell you."

"I'm very pleased with our decision," Jack said, squeezing Ivy's hand. "We'll be back later."

"What kind of museum are you going to?" Melissa asked. She and Scott looked better than everyone else, although they didn't look particularly happy with one another. Ivy was starting to wonder if they ever smiled when they were together.

"It's some dead animal museum with a great gift shop," Jack said, grinning. "I have no idea. Ivy described it and it sounded just kitschy enough to be fun."

"Can we go with you?" Melissa asked. "I would love to get out of here for a few hours."

"Oh ... um ... ."

"I think they want to be alone so they can gaze at each other adoringly," Donnie interjected.

"Oh, I'm sorry," Melissa said, her face falling.

"No, it's fine," Jack said, exchanging a quick look with Ivy. "We don't mind."

"We'd be happy for the company," Ivy said, offering Melissa a warm smile. "Although, I'm not sure the museum we're visiting is going to be quite what you expect."

"Anything is better than sitting around a campfire all day," Melissa said. "Give me five minutes to change."

"HOLY CRAP!" Scott's eyes widened as the foursome sauntered into the Call of the Wild lobby an hour later. "This is ... there are no words."

Jack followed his gaze, not bothering to hide his smile as he took in the huge room. There were shelves on almost every wall, each laden with trinkets he couldn't quite believe he was seeing. He reached toward the one closest to him and grabbed a raccoon hat – complete with tail – and held it up. "I've always wanted one of these."

Ivy smirked. "I told you the gift shop was something to behold," she said. "You have to go through the museum before you shop, though."

"Oh, come on," Jack protested. "They have deer antlers on a felt-covered board over there."

"I think they have voodoo dolls over here," Melissa said, her eyes sparkling as she held up a small poppet. "It looks like a witch."

"You have to go through the museum first." Ivy was firm. "That's the way it's done. Come on. I promise you're going to find the museum just as cool as the gift shop."

"I think you're playing me, but I'm dying to see it," Jack said, digging into his wallet and handing two twenties to the woman behind the counter. "We need four tickets to the museum."

Since she'd been there before, Ivy led the way to the museum, pushing through the glass doors and ushering Jack, Scott, and Melissa into a strange new world. The walls were cement and arched, almost as if they were walking through a cave, and even though the museum was almost completely empty, it felt like coming home to Ivy.

"I'm already sold on this," Jack said, laughing as he ran his hand over the wall. "What's with the paw prints on the floor?" He pointed toward the brown prints.

"You follow them to get through the museum," Ivy answered.

"Of course," Jack said, grabbing Ivy's hand and pulling her forward so he could study the first display. It was a gray wolf on a lonely country road. "Maybe he's your dogman."

"Don't push me on that, Jack," Ivy warned.

"That's a real animal carcass," Melissa said, wrinkling her nose. "Did they kill it just for this museum?"

"No," Ivy replied, shaking her head. "Most of the animals here were hit by cars or killed a very long time ago. I wouldn't come here if they were killing animals simply so they could display them."

"I think it's cool," Scott said, leaning forward. "This place is neat. What's next?"

Jack chuckled. "I would think this is below your refined taste," he said.

"No way," Scott said. "You never get to see this type of stuff where we live. You have to embrace it when you can."

"Lead the way, Ivy," Jack prodded.

Ivy didn't need to be told twice. She gladly directed everyone through the museum, laughing maniacally when Jack got distracted by one of the Native American exhibits. It had a weird projector that superimposed a talking face on a dummy, recounting some Michigan settlement story for everyone to giggle at. Even though she'd been looking forward to an afternoon alone with Jack, Ivy found she didn't mind Melissa and Scott's company. Away from the group, they were almost charming.

"Okay, I'm so glad we did that," Jack said when they emerged from the museum. "I'm going to torture you for months with all that stuff, honey. You know that, right?"

"You can't torture me with this museum," Ivy countered. "I love it too much."

"Can we shop now?" Melissa asked, her eyes sparkling. "I want to go over every inch of this gift shop. Not only is it cool, but I think there are probably treasures here that people would never dream of discovering."

"There are actually some really cool things here," Ivy agreed.

They split up into couples, Jack and Ivy moving along the outer shelves while Scott and Melissa hit the inner ones. Ivy watched them for a moment, smiling as they chatted amiably to one another. When she turned back to Jack, he was watching her.

"What?"

"Why are you staring at them?" Jack asked.

"If you must know, I was a little worried that they hated each other until I saw them on their own today," Ivy admitted. "They seem okay now, but they barely look at each other at the campground."

"Do you know why that is?"

Ivy shook her head, following Jack as he checked out the miniature car replicas.

"It's because Maria stirs all the women up every chance she gets," Jack supplied, his voice low. "She gets off on the drama. I'm sure you've noticed."

"She seems ... nice," Ivy said, choosing her words carefully.

"I don't really like Maria, so feel free to be honest," Jack said.

"Okay, she's obnoxious," Ivy conceded. "Why did Alex marry her?"

Jack shrugged. "I think he loved her," he answered. "I think he probably still loves her. She's just very … set in her ways. She's a hard person to like."

"Do you think I'm going to be that way one day?" Ivy asked, genuinely curious. "Are you worried I'm going to be hard to like down the road?"

"No, honey, I don't worry about that at all," Jack said. "You're stubborn … like a mule. I would be lying if I said otherwise. You're also loving, giving, and a great listener. Maria is none of those things. Just because you're stubborn, that doesn't mean you're unlikeable. In fact, I like everything about you … including that stubborn streak."

Ivy's cheeks burned, pleasure washing over her. "Thank you."

"And that right there is something that Maria would never do," Jack said, kissing Ivy's cheek and tweaking her nose. "Don't worry about things that are never going to happen, Ivy. Worry about things that could happen … like me buying one of those raccoon hats so I can wear it while we're … napping."

"I'm not napping with you if you have that on," Ivy shot back. "You've been warned. If you buy one of those hats I'm going to … ." Ivy mimed choking him, causing Jack to snicker.

"I'm going back to look at them," Jack said. "I don't care what you say. I think I would look great in one of those hats."

"Knock yourself out," Ivy said. "I'm going to check out the hand-blown glass stuff. They usually have unique items."

"I won't leave without you," Jack said. "Mostly because I know I would be sad and cry if I did."

"You *are* whipped," Ivy teased.

"And proud of it," Jack said, poking her side before ambling back in the direction of the raccoon hats.

Ivy allowed the warmth of Jack's previous words to wash over her as she headed for her favorite corner of the gift shop. While communication wasn't always easy for them, Jack was getting better and better at verbalizing his feelings. It left her feeling happy and delighted as she perused the gift offerings.

"You look happy," Scott said, appearing at Ivy's side and causing her to jolt. She almost dropped the hummingbird feeder in her hand, but regained herself and caught it before it could crash to the floor.

"You shouldn't sneak up on people when they're holding expensive glass items," Ivy chided, placing the feeder back on the shelf and exhaling heavily.

"Sorry about that," Scott said, smiling. "That's pretty. You should get it. It's almost as pretty as you."

Ivy forced a smile, but Scott's strange words – and nervous demeanor – made her uncomfortable. "I don't really need a humming-bird feeder, but thank you." Ivy moved to the other side of the shelf, hoping Scott would take the hint and leave her to browse in peace, but she wasn't that lucky.

"I'm glad you and Jack found each other," Scott said, his eyes fixated on the high ridges of Ivy's cheekbones as he watched her look over the glass animal menagerie. "We were really worried about him after the shooting."

"Jack made it through that on his own," Ivy said. "He's very strong. He was already finding himself when he came to Shadow Lake."

"And you helped him along the rest of the way," Scott surmised.

"We helped each other," Ivy countered. "Jack is the best man I know. You're lucky to have him as a friend."

"Of course I'm lucky to have Jack as a friend," Scott scoffed. "He's a great guy. You have to understand, though, we were all worried Jack was going to do something to hurt himself because he was so upset by what his partner did.

"His recovery was slow and painful," he continued. "There were days I thought he was going to eat his gun just to get away from the memories."

Ivy frowned. While Jack didn't confide in her when he first came to town, he never once struck her as suicidal. In fact, deep down inside, Ivy knew that no matter what happened there was nothing that would make Jack take the easy way out. Scott suggesting otherwise was both irritating and baffling.

"Jack would never do that," Ivy argued. "He was coming to grips with what happened when he came to town. He needed to get some perspective, and he couldn't do that in the city. He would never hurt himself, though."

"Well, we'll have to agree to disagree," Scott said. "I think I know Jack better than you."

"I don't think you know Jack at all if you believe that," Ivy shot back, moving around the shelf again. She needed distance from Scott. If he wasn't careful, she was going to smack him in the head with the hummingbird feeder and then gladly pay for the ruined mess on her way out the door.

"I think you're very good for Jack," Scott said. "He needed something to get him out of his funk. The fact that you came along to do it, well, even if this is just a fling, I think you've been very good for him."

"A fling?"

"You know what I mean," Scott said. "Eventually Jack is going to move back to the city. A guy like him is never going to be happy in a place the size of Shadow Lake. I get the feeling you wouldn't be happy in a city. So … ."

"So you think Jack is just sleeping with me until he gets bored of Shadow Lake," Ivy surmised.

"That's not a bad thing," Scott said hurriedly. "You're a beautiful woman. Men will be falling all over you to take a crack once you're single again. I can't think of anyone – and I do mean anyone – who wouldn't want you."

Ivy took an inadvertent step away from Scott, licking her lips as she decided how to answer. She didn't get the chance because Jack picked that moment to return.

"I decided against the hat," Jack said. "I figured you would never have sex with me again if I bought it."

"Pretty much," Ivy agreed, forcing her gaze in his direction. "Are you ready to go?"

"Have you looked around the store? I haven't seen you leave this area. We have time if you want to shop."

"We can come back another day," Ivy said, moving away from Scott. "I don't really want to shop right now."

Jack watched her go, confused, and then shifted his eyes to Scott. "What did you say to her?"

"I didn't say anything," Scott protested. "Why do you think that?"

"Because she wasn't upset five minutes ago, and she's clearly upset now," Jack answered. "What did you say to her? Before you try to think up a lie, by the way, she's going to tell me the truth once we're alone, so be very careful how you answer."

"I just suggested that this relationship can't last because you'll eventually move back down to the city and she'll stay up here," Scott said, flinching at the murderous look moving across Jack's face. "I'm … sorry."

"First of all, where I live is none of your concern," Jack hissed. "Second of all, Shadow Lake is my home now. Ivy is my home. Even if Ivy didn't exist, though, I wouldn't move back to the city. It doesn't hold any appeal. Not now. I'm done with the city."

"I'm sorry," Scott said. "I just thought … ."

"I don't care what you thought," Jack said. "Don't ever say anything like that to Ivy again. I mean it."

"Is that a threat?"

"I don't care how you take it," Jack said. "You're my friend, but you're not my keeper. You're from my past and I like keeping in touch, but if I have to cut you loose I'll do it. She's my present, and I'm very hopeful that she's going to be my future. Don't ever say anything like that to her again."

Nine

"Ivy, let's talk," Jack said a few hours later, shooting a dark look in Scott's direction before following her into their tent. Lunch was a somber affair, and Melissa couldn't help but notice that everyone seemed silent and angry. No one would explain what happened, though, and everyone was eager to return to camp so they could get away from one another.

"There's nothing to talk about, Jack," Ivy said, plopping down on the sleeping bags and yanking her shoes off. "I'm fine."

"You're not fine," Jack argued, joining her. "I asked Scott what he said to you, and I'm not at all happy with what he told me. I warned him not to say anything like that to you again."

"Great. Thank you."

Jack didn't appreciate Ivy's clipped tone. "Would you feel better if I went out there and beat him up? Because I'll do it."

Despite herself, Ivy couldn't stop herself from chuckling. "I don't think that will be necessary."

"Honey, I'm sorry for what he said." Jack brushed Ivy's hair away from her face so he could study her angular features. "You know I'm not leaving Shadow Lake, though. We've already discussed it. You don't have to worry about that."

"Is that all he told you he said?"

Jack faltered. "Why? What else did he say?"

"I'm not going to lie, Jack," Ivy said. "He's odd."

"Okay, tell me what he said right now," Jack instructed. "I'm definitely going to beat his ass if I don't like it."

"He said that he was glad we found each other because they were all worried you were going to kill yourself after the shooting," Ivy answered, her heart sinking as Jack's face hardened.

"What?"

Ivy grabbed Jack's hand to reassure him. "I told him that you would never do anything like that, and he said that I didn't know you as well as he did and that essentially I had no idea what I was talking about."

"You know that's not true, right?" Jack asked, pressing the heel of his hand against his forehead. "I wouldn't do that, no matter how unhappy I was."

"I know."

"I don't understand why he would say that to you," Jack muttered. "What was he trying to accomplish?"

"I'm not sure," Ivy hedged. "He also said that I was a beautiful woman and that any man – and he stressed the word 'any' – would love to spend time with me. To be honest, it made me a little uncomfortable."

"Do you think he was hitting on you?"

Ivy shrugged. "I don't know."

"Well, I'm definitely going to have to beat him," Jack said, moving to get off the cushion. "I have no idea what got into him, but I'm not putting up with that."

"No," Ivy said, grabbing Jack around the waist and wrestling him back onto the sleeping bags. "Don't do that."

Jack rolled to his side and locked gazes with Ivy. "Why?"

"I don't want this week to be ruined because your friend is a jerk," Ivy explained. "I want to have fun. If you go out there and fight with him, everyone is going to pick sides – and they're going to look at me as the enemy.

"Now, granted, I don't particularly see myself being friends with these people over the long haul," she continued. "If we can get through this week, though, you can still have your long-distance friendship with them. That's important to you."

"You're more important," Jack said, rubbing his thumb against Ivy's cheek as he pulled her closer and rested his head on the pillows. "Ivy, I'm not going to let Scott make you feel uneasy. That's not who I am."

"Have you considered that maybe he was testing me?"

"How does that work?"

"I don't know," Ivy replied. "Maybe he was purposely saying stuff to see if he could get me to talk badly about you."

"That sounds like something chicks do," Jack argued. "Grown men don't do things like that."

"I don't want you to fight with him because of me."

Her face was so earnest Jack couldn't muster the energy to argue with her. "If he says something to you again, you need to tell me."

"I promise."

"Then I guess I'll let it go," Jack said, cuddling Ivy close and pressing a soft kiss to her forehead. "I don't want to fight. I was looking forward to this trip as much as you were."

"I'm sorry things haven't been going as well as you hoped," Ivy offered. "When was the last time you saw them?"

"Everyone came to the hospital after I was shot," Jack answered, stroking the back of Ivy's head. "I wasn't in a good place, although I was not contemplating suicide. I have no idea where Scott got that idea."

"Jack, you don't have to worry about me believing that," Ivy said. "I knew from the moment I met you that you weren't the type of person who could do anything of the sort."

"Do you know that I'm never going back to the city?"

Ivy bit her lip and nodded. "I was worried when I found out you still had a house in Detroit," she admitted. "Once you told me that you put it on the market, though, I knew you were okay staying in Shadow Lake."

"Honey, I'm more than okay staying in Shadow Lake," Jack said. "I like the town. I like how wide open it feels. I don't want to bruise your ego, but it's not just you keeping me in Shadow Lake."

"Oh, well, now you tell."

"You make me very happy, Ivy," Jack said. "Even before I was shot, there was no happiness in that city. Not as far as I was concerned, at least. The job was all I had there, and after I was shot I realized that wasn't enough. I have found a lot of happiness in Shadow Lake, and you're only part of it."

Ivy slipped her arm around Jack's waist and edged closer. "I'm glad you found happiness in Shadow Lake," she said. "I think you should tell me all the things I do to make you happy, though. Forget all that other stuff."

Jack chuckled as he rubbed her back. "I'm only doing this for one reason. You know that, right?"

Ivy nodded. "You're doing it because you're hoping to lull me into another nap when you're done."

"You are the smartest woman in the world."

"I have my moments."

BY THE TIME DINNER ROLLED AROUND, JACK AND IVY DECIDED to rejoin the group – although Jack stuck close to her and offered his help so they could cook together. Ivy pulled a marinated steak out of a baggie and put it in the cast iron skillet so she could roast it, leaving Jack to spear vegetables on skewers for kebabs. He didn't move his eyes from her as she worked on the far side of the campfire.

"Do you want to tell me what happened?" Alex asked, popping the tab on a beer and settling next to Jack. "The four of you have been very quiet since you got back from your museum trip."

"It's not important," Jack replied.

"It seems important," Alex countered. "You and Ivy spent the entire afternoon in your tent while Scott paced and muttered to himself out here. Tell me."

"He said some things to Ivy and I'm ticked off," Jack said. "Even if he believed what he said – and I'm having a hard time fathoming how he could – he should have kept his big, fat mouth shut."

"What did he say?"

"He told her that I was using her for sex and planned on taking off to the city once I was done with her," Jack answered, rolling his neck until it cracked. "He also told her he was glad she found me when she did because he was convinced I was going to kill myself."

Alex stilled, surprised. "What?"

"You heard me."

"I can't believe he said that to her," Alex said. "You know he was really worried about that, though, right?"

"I don't see why," Jack replied. "I would never kill myself."

"We weren't so sure about that," Alex said. "You were in a really ... bad ... place after the shooting. You wouldn't talk to anyone. Your mother had to force you to eat. You went weeks without talking to people and never left your house. I know you don't want to hear it, but we were all worried."

"That's all well and good, but I would never kill myself and for him to say something like that to Ivy ... ."

"It's obvious how you feel about Ivy, and I couldn't be happier for you," Alex said. "He definitely shouldn't have said anything to her, but she's a big girl. Something tells me she can take him if it comes to a fight."

Jack snorted. "She's the strongest person I know."

"Then I guess that makes you the strongest couple I know," Alex said. "Don't let Scott get to you. He's having issues with Melissa. I'm sure you've seen how they interact. That marriage is not going to survive."

"They seemed fine at the museum, happy even."

"Well, I don't think that's a normal occurrence in their marriage," Alex supplied. "Just, don't let it get to you. Scott is miserable and you're happy. He's probably jealous."

"If he says anything else to her, I'm going to beat him," Jack warned. "You share the message."

"I'll get right on that."

"THAT WAS THE BEST STEAK I'VE EVER HAD," JACK SAID FORTY

minutes later, cleaning his plate and expectantly turning toward Ivy. "How come you never grilled steak for me before?"

"You know how I feel about dead cow."

"I do," Jack said. "That's why I'm baffled that you know how to cook it."

"I looked it up online before we left," Ivy said, grabbing his plate so she could secure their garbage and keep it away from scavengers.

"You looked up how to make a steak for me online and then sat there and ate two skewers of vegetables," Jack said. "Somehow that doesn't seem fair."

"I happen to like vegetables."

"I happen to like you," Jack said, grabbing her around the waist and pulling her close so he could kiss her. "How about we go to bed early tonight? We can look through the hole in the roof and stargaze."

"What about your friends?" Ivy kept her voice low. "I think they've figured out that something is going on."

"I don't really care about them right now," Jack said, shifting a quick look in their direction and finding six faces staring back at him. "I kind of feel like an animal at the zoo."

"I have a better idea," Ivy said. "Let's take a walk around the campground so our dinner can digest – and you can make sure you're nice and calm – and then we'll come back to the fire for an hour and *then* we'll go to bed and look at the stars."

"I will only agree to that if you're naked for the stargazing."

"Deal," Ivy said, rolling to the balls of her feet so she could kiss his cheek. "I'll tell everyone where we're going. You ... wait here."

"Yes ma'am," Jack teased, kicking his heels together as he mock saluted. He watched Ivy approach the group and explain what they were doing, Scott's eyes traveling toward him across the expanse. Jack had no idea what the man was thinking, his face was unreadable, but he was still angry about what he said to Ivy. Jack was so caught up watching the scene play out that he didn't notice two park rangers approaching until they were almost on top of him.

"What's going on?" Jack asked, lifting his eyebrows.

"We're looking for a teenage girl," one of the rangers said, holding out a photograph so Jack could study it. "Her name is Kylie Bradford. Have you seen her?"

Jack shook his head. "I haven't, but we should see if the others have," he said, carrying the photograph closer to the fire. "Only half of us were here today. We went to Gaylord for the afternoon."

"The girl has been missing since last night. She disappeared from her tent in the overnight hours."

"What's going on?" Donnie asked, getting to his feet.

"There's a missing teenager," Jack said, showing the photograph to Ivy first and then handing it to his friends so they could pass it around. "Has anyone seen her?"

"I haven't," Maria replied. "To be fair, though, we haven't been paying attention to the other campers. I'm sorry."

"This is kind of a reunion for us," Scott interjected. "We're in our own little world."

"You say she's been gone since last night?" Ivy asked, earning a nod in return. "Was she here with friends?"

"She was here with her parents and siblings," the ranger replied. "They're freaking out. We're hopeful she just met up with some other teenagers and got drunk or something. Maybe she's hiding because she doesn't want to get in trouble."

"We can help you look around," Jack offered. "I'm a detective with the Shadow Lake Police Department. This is a lot of ground to cover. I can make a copy of the photograph with my phone and ask people."

"That would be a big help."

"We'll all help," Scott said, moving closer to Jack. "The women can stay here so no one gets lost, but we'll go out and see if we can find her."

"I guess we're all going," Jack said, exchanging a quick look with Ivy. "We'll start right now."

Ten

Ivy didn't put up a fight when Jack left without her. She thought time alone with Scott would do him some good. While Melissa, Maria, and Lauren returned to their conversation as if nothing was out of the ordinary, Ivy couldn't engage. Something was wrong. She could feel it.

After a few minutes of restless pacing, an idea nudged at the edges of Ivy's mind and she had a sickening thought. She glanced at the sun, frowning when she realized how close it was to setting, and then moved to leave the campsite.

"Tell Jack I'll be back as soon as I can," she called over her shoulder.

"Where are you going?" Maria asked.

"I just … there was a clearing in the woods not far away and I want to check it out," Ivy answered. "If Jack beats me back, tell him that's where I went and I'll be fine. Don't let him go looking for me. He might get lost."

"I think you should stay here," Maria said. "They didn't look like they wanted our help."

"I think you should ask Jack before you go running off into the woods," Lauren added.

"I don't need Jack's permission," Ivy replied, moving into the forest without a backward glance. She knew exactly where she was heading, and she had a feeling she was going to find something awful when she got there.

"**WHERE** is Ivy?" Jack asked, glancing around the campsite an hour later, his face unreadable. After a few tense moments with his friends as they moved between campsites, Scott apologized for what he said and admitted he was out of line. Jack wasn't thrilled with any of it, but he opted to make amends instead of dwelling on it. He was here to have a good time, and he wasn't going to let Scott ruin things, no matter how misguided his notions were.

"She took off into the woods about five minutes after you left," Maria answered. "She seemed determined to look in some clearing you guys found yesterday. We told her not to go."

"I told her she should ask you before going, but she said she didn't need your permission," Lauren added.

"I am going to kill her," Jack hissed, turning toward the trees. "I am just ... she is unbelievable!"

"Chill out, man," Donnie said, grabbing Jack's arm before he could storm off. "It's almost dark. You shouldn't go out there. You'll get lost."

"She said to tell you not to go looking for her," Melissa offered. "She said she would be fine on her own."

"She's not fine on her own," Jack said, jerking his arm away from Donnie. "I am going to ... ."

"We'll go with you," Scott said, holding his hands up in a placating manner. "I'm sure she's fine."

"She had better be," Jack said, moving toward his tent. "We have flashlights. I need to grab them."

"We'll be waiting."

IVY knew what she was going to find before she walked into the clearing. She had no idea how she knew, but dread filled her chest and threatened to smother her as she moved closer to the large rock.

The light was dim, but Ivy could make out the silhouette of a body – at least she thought it was a body. She couldn't be sure because what was left was ... mangled. She opened her mouth to yell, realizing almost immediately it would be fruitless. There was no one close enough to hear her scream. She pulled her cell phone out of her pocket and sighed when she saw two bars. She dialed 911 and pressed the phone to her ear, sucking in a deep breath before the operator picked up.

"What's your emergency?"

"I just found a dead body," Ivy replied, hoping she sounded calm instead of hysterical. She was bordering on the latter. "I need the police out here right now."

JACK HEARD THE SOUND OF VOICES BEFORE HE SAW THE flashlight beams bouncing between the trees. He increased his pace, ignoring Donnie's mumbled worries about tripping, and bolted through the tree line, pulling up short when he saw Ivy standing next to a state police officer.

She lifted her eyes, as if sensing him, and threw herself in his arms as he approached. "I found her."

"I am going to kill you for taking off on me," Jack said, smoothing down her hair. There wasn't a lot of heft behind his words. "You scared me. You need to stop doing that."

"I'm sorry," Ivy said, wiping a stray tear from her cheek as she pulled away. "I just ... I had to check. You were already gone. I figured I was imagining things and that I would beat you back to camp."

"Well, you didn't," Jack said, turning his attention to the trooper. "I'm Jack Harker. I'm a detective in Shadow Lake. What's the situation?"

"I'm Tad Harvey," the trooper replied. "Ms. Morgan called 911 after discovering the body. She had to meet us out on the highway and lead us back to this location because she couldn't direct us without landmarks. We believe we've discovered the remains of a teenage girl."

"You believe? How come you don't know?"

"The remains are ... not complete," Harvey replied.

"I don't understand what that means," Jack said, casting a glance over his shoulder to make sure Donnie, Scott, and Alex were safely ensconced in the clearing but out of the way of law enforcement at the same time.

"She was shredded," Ivy answered. "Her ... face ... was missing. Something tore out her stomach, too."

"How long did you spend looking at the body before you called us?" Harvey asked.

Ivy balked. "Not long. I ... you could see what happened to her right away."

"And you don't know the deceased, correct?"

"What are you asking?" Jack interrupted, slipping his arm over Ivy's shoulders to lend her a little bit of his warmth. She'd taken off into the woods without bothering to grab a hoodie or long pants.

"Ms. Morgan discovered a body in the middle of the woods," Harvey said. "She claims she had a feeling the body might be here because the two of you discovered the clearing yesterday. I have trouble believing she's ... psychic."

"I didn't say I was psychic," Ivy protested. "I said I thought the clearing might make a nice place for teenagers to congregate away from their parents. That's what I was checking for when I came out here."

"And I'm sure you understand that I have to check every possible angle," Harvey countered. "Can you tell me where you were between the hours of midnight and six o'clock this morning?"

"In my tent."

"Can anyone vouch for you?" Harvey pressed.

"I can," Jack volunteered.

"You were with Ms. Morgan the entire night?"

"I was," Jack answered. "We're sleeping in the same tent. Heck, we're sleeping in the same sleeping bag. She was with me all of that time."

"And you're sure she didn't sneak out while you were sleeping?"

"I'm sure because we woke up twice during the night and ... did something else," Jack responded.

Ivy was glad it was dark out so Harvey couldn't see the blush creeping up her cheeks.

"I see," Harvey said. "And you didn't know the deceased either, did you, Detective Harker?"

"I've never laid eyes on her before," Jack said. "In fact, the rangers came to our campsite and showed a photo and we went around asking other campers if they saw her earlier this evening. That's where I was when Ivy decided to go walking through woods alone."

"Thank you for answering our questions," Harvey said, his tone cool. "We'll be in touch."

Jack arched a challenging eyebrow. "That's it?"

"That's it," Harvey said. "We need you to vacate the premises. This is an active crime scene now."

"I'm looking forward to it," Jack muttered, grabbing Ivy's hand and dragging her away from the trooper. "You're in a lot of trouble, missy."

"I KNOW YOU'RE ANGRY, BUT CAN WE PLEASE NOT FIGHT?" Ivy asked a half hour later, stripping out of her shirt and shorts and settling on the sleeping bags. "I'm not sure I can take it."

"I'm sorry you're upset, and we're going to talk about that in a minute, but we're fighting first," Jack said. "What were you thinking?"

"I knew, Jack," Ivy said, her voice trembling. "All of sudden ... I just knew."

Jack's expression softened. "Honey, I'm sorry this happened to you," he said, settling next to her and wrapping his arm around her back. "I know you must be shaken up. That still doesn't justify you taking off into the woods when it was almost dark. You had to know that would drive me crazy."

"I had to see. The clearing was ... calling to me ... just like before."

Jack restlessly tugged a hand through his hair. "Ivy, look at me."

Ivy didn't immediately react or respond, so Jack tilted her chin so she had no choice but to meet his somber gaze.

"Ivy, I can't lose you," Jack said. "I just got you. You should have called me on my phone ... or waited for me to get back ... or just about anything else other than what you did. Tell me you know what you did was wrong."

"I know I shouldn't have gone out there on my own," Ivy confirmed. "I honestly couldn't help myself. I ... you should've seen her, Jack. If it wasn't for the clothing, I'm not sure I wouldn't have thought it was an animal carcass when I first saw it."

"Okay," Jack said, pulling the edge of the sleeping bag down and motioning for Ivy to crawl inside. He climbed in after her, killing the lantern light and then carefully pulled her on top of him. "Walk me through it, honey. Tell me what made you run into the woods, and then tell me what you saw. I know it's hard, but the faster you get through it, the faster we can go to a happy place in our dreams. I need to know, though."

"The other women were talking by the fire, and I remember being really annoyed because I didn't understand how they could sit there talking about whichever Kardashian was breaking up this week when a teenage girl was missing," Ivy said.

"You're not a fan of useless conversation," Jack said. "Then what happened?"

"I don't know," Ivy answered. "I felt like this ... prick ... on the back of my neck, and the clearing jumped into my head. I knew."

"Tell me what happened when you got to the clearing," Jack prodded.

"For some reason I knew she was by the rock," Ivy said. "I walked in that direction and I realized what I was looking at even before I saw the clothing. I knew it was a body, but even then I couldn't quite figure out what I was looking at because the flesh was ... mangled.

"Then I saw the blond hair," she continued. "I realized that what I was looking at was the spot where her face was supposed to be. It wasn't there. Neither was her stomach."

"Okay," Jack said, rubbing Ivy's back as he shifted her closer. She was shaking. "That's it. We're done talking about it. Try taking a few deep breaths and relax. You need sleep. I'm worried you're in shock."

"Something tore her apart, Jack," Ivy said.

"Do you think it was an animal? You said bears could be in the area. Could a bear do that?"

"Bears don't attack people unless they're backed into a corner or protecting their young."

"What if it was rabid?"

"We would've heard about rabies running through the area," Ivy replied. "I remember one or two instances of that being a thing, and everyone was put on alert. We would know before this because a smaller animal would've attacked closer to a house."

"We don't know anything yet, honey," Jack said, tightening the covers around them as he tried to keep Ivy warm. "She could've fallen and hit her head. Scavengers might have eaten her body if they happened upon it."

"Or someone killed her."

"That's a possibility," Jack conceded, refusing to lie to her even though she was mired in a fragile mental state. "I want you to try and push it out of your mind, though. We're going to a happy place in our dreams tonight."

"How do you know we'll dream walk? We don't do it every night."

"Because I can't be separated from you right now," Jack replied, opting for honesty. "I think we both know we're going to find each other tonight. So, I'm going to pick the destination. How does Disney World sound?"

"I don't care where we go," Ivy said. "I just … make it someplace bright."

"Your wish is my command," Jack said, pressing a kiss to Ivy's forehead. "Try to relax. Try to sleep. I'll be right here. I promise. We'll be together."

Jack held on long enough to be sure Ivy had drifted off, and then he joined her in a happy place. He couldn't eradicate all of her fears, but he could put on a brave front and show her a good time.

For now, that was all he could do. He just hoped it was enough.

Eleven

✿

"How are things?" Donnie asked, his eyes falling on Jack and Ivy as they exited their tent the next morning.

"They're fine," Jack said, keeping his hand at Ivy's waist as they moved toward the picnic table. "Sorry we slept so late, but we were tired."

"I'll bet," Maria said. "How weird was it to find that body yesterday, Ivy? Was it gross?"

Jack scowled as Alex flicked Maria's ear to quiet her. "Don't ask her about that," Jack ordered. "I'm serious."

"It's fine," Ivy said, offering Jack a watery smile before moving toward their cooler. "We need to pick up another bag of ice today, by the way. They sell them up at the ranger cabin."

"I'll get one," Jack said, watching as she pulled a baggie full of already whipped eggs and chopped vegetables out of the cooler. "Why don't you let me cook today?"

"Because I'm capable of cooking breakfast myself," Ivy replied. "There's some sausage in there for you to go with your omelet, by the way."

"You bought me sausage, too?" Jack was impressed. "You really are my favorite person ever."

Ivy snorted, offering Jack a glimpse of the first real smile she'd mustered since the previous evening. He was relieved, although he didn't voice his happiness out loud. "You can cook your own sausage, if that will make you happy."

"I love sausage, so I will gladly cook it," Jack said, narrowing his eyes as he regarded the fire. "How do you suggest I cook it if you're using the skillet?"

"You know those long forks I bought and you thought I was going to poke you with them?"

"Ah," Jack said, realization dawning. "You are a very bright woman." He dropped a quick kiss on her forehead. "How much sausage can I have?"

"I bought it all for you," Ivy replied. "I would hope you don't have enough to give yourself a heart attack from all that grease, but other than that, the decision is completely yours."

"Will we run out?"

"There's bacon in there for you, too."

"Yup, you're my favorite person ever," Jack said, leaving Ivy with her omelet ingredients and moving closer to the fire with his sausage and metal prong. He sat between Donnie and Alex so he could keep an eye on Ivy, offering each of his friends a small nod before turning to his task. "Have you guys heard anything?" Jack purposely kept his voice low.

"We talked to a few other campers before you guys got up," Donnie said. "No one was up late last night because ... well ... we just weren't. You guys slept longer than we expected, though."

"She was worked up and needed to calm down before she could fall asleep," Jack said.

"Is she okay?"

"The body was chewed up," Jack replied. "She saw it. Apparently the girl's face was gone. She's ... shaken."

"That's horrible," Scott said. "What do you think happened?"

"I have no idea," Jack answered. "For all we know she could've tripped, hit her head, and accidentally died. She could also have been murdered."

"For what it's worth, the rangers are saying that they can't find any wounds on her body that would suggest murder," Alex said. "It very well could be an accident."

"That would be nice," Jack said, shoving the prong through two sausage links. "The problem is, Ivy said the body was so messed up she would've mistaken it for an animal carcass at first glance. The girl's face and stomach were gone, and Ivy can't be sure if more of her was missing because she stopped looking when she realized all of that blond hair was attached to what should've been a head."

"How can you say things like that while cooking sausage?" Donnie asked, making a face.

"I guess I'm used to it," Jack said. "I didn't even think about it."

"Do the cops suspect Ivy?" Scott asked. "We couldn't hear everything you guys were talking about last night, but you didn't seem happy with whatever was being said."

"The trooper questioning her wanted to know where we were the previous night," Jack said. "That's standard for any investigation. I still didn't like his attitude. If she was a murderer, why would she call for help after discovering the body? Why would she go back at all? She has absolutely no motive. He was just talking to hear himself talk."

"Plus, she's too cute to be a murderer," Alex said, grinning.

"I honestly hope we find out it was some sort of accident," Jack said. "I want to keep her busy today, though. She's still kind of ... shaky. I was thinking we could go kayaking. I've never been in one before and I'm sure I'll end up in the water. That should make her laugh because she's a pro."

"Does she kayak a lot?"

"She and Max go whenever they can," Jack said. "I think she's been holding back since we started dating. We spend our weekends holed up in her house and shut out the world these days, but I know she's pretty good. Apparently she and Max hold competitions, and she regularly beats him."

"Is Max a big guy?"

"He's pretty big, and he works out five days a week," Jack said. "He always throws that in my face when I threaten to beat him up."

"It sounds like you've picked up a girlfriend and a brother," Donnie said, his eyes twinkling. "You have a whole new family."

"I guess I do," Jack said.

"Are you happy about that?"

"I haven't ever been this happy," Jack replied. "I want to make sure Ivy has at least a little fun today. So, is everyone okay with kayaking?"

"I'm looking forward to it," Donnie said. "Now that I know you've never done it before, I can't wait to tip you over."

"Don't think I won't beat you," Jack warned. "That will probably make Ivy laugh, too."

"I'll take that under consideration."

"SO, WAIT ... WHAT DO YOU WANT ME TO DO?"

Jack balanced the double-edged paddle across the kayak opening and watched Ivy demonstrate with her own paddle.

"You're holding it backward," Ivy said. "Turn it this way." She shifted it and then pressed it back into his hands. "Do you see how that dips down there? That's the end you want pointing into the water. You'll get blisters on your hands if you hold it the other way."

"This looks complicated," Jack said.

Ivy stood next to his kayak, the water coming to just above her knees, and fixed him with an exasperated look. "I want you to enjoy this," she said. "If you do, we can go out together sometimes. It's a great workout."

"I believe you," Jack said. "I'm just not convinced I won't tip over ... and if I do, those jackholes are going to laugh at me." He inclined his chin in Donnie and Alex's direction, his friends laughing as they bent their heads together about twenty feet farther out.

"I'm glad you're using the word jackholes to describe people," Ivy said. "Now you can't yell at me when I do it."

"I still think we need to come up with a better word," Jack grumbled.

"Jack, this isn't a canoe," Ivy explained. "You're an athlete. You already have good balance. It's much easier to tip over in a canoe when you have multiple people distributing their weight in uneven patterns. Even if you do tip over, though, it's going to be okay. I promise not to laugh at you."

"You can laugh at me," Jack offered. "I would tip myself over to see that right now."

"I'll see what I can do," Ivy said. "Why don't you try paddling out to Donnie and Alex? I'll get my kayak together and meet you out there in a few minutes. We won't move too far away from shore to start things off."

"Okay," Jack said. "Give me a kiss first."

Ivy leaned forward and did as instructed. "You're going to be fine."

"You know they're going to try and tip me over, right?"

"Don't worry about that," Ivy said. "I can guarantee I'm better in a kayak than either of them. I'll take them out if it becomes necessary."

"Yup, you're still my favorite person in the world."

Ivy watched Jack paddle toward his friends, lightly chuckling as he tried to get a handle on how to work the paddle. She couldn't wait to take him down a river. That would be a whole new set of problems, and yet more fun at the same time. She enjoyed kayaking on a lake, but she absolutely adored doing it on a river.

Ivy turned her attention back to the shore so she could gather her kayak and stilled when she found Scott watching her. "Do you need something?"

"To apologize," Scott said, not missing a beat. "I've been waiting for a chance to get you alone so I could do it, but after last night … um … it just didn't happen in a timely fashion."

"You don't need to apologize to me," Ivy countered. "Apologize to Jack. He's the one who was upset."

"I think you were upset, too," Scott said. "For the record, I apologized to Jack last night. We made up while we were out taking that photograph around and looking for the girl."

"I'm glad," Ivy said. "I think your friendship with Jack is important to him."

"Listen, what I said to you yesterday was uncalled for," Scott said. "I don't have a good excuse. Melissa and I have been fighting nonstop, and I was looking forward to seeing Jack because I thought he was single and it would give me a chance to get away from my wife."

"I'm not sure you should be telling me this," Ivy said, shifting from one foot to the other as she grabbed the front end of her kayak and leveraged it into the water. "It's really none of my business."

"I'm not trying to be one of those crazy oversharers, if that's what you're thinking," Scott said. "Jack was alone for a long time. I was hoping he would be able to convince me I could be alone.

"When I saw how happy he was with you, it kind of threw me for a loop," he continued. "I just … Jack has never been as close to a woman as he is with you. It freaked me out a little bit."

"I understand that change is hard for you guys because you've known each other for so long," Ivy said. "I just want Jack to be happy."

"You make him happy," Scott said. "Heck, you would make anyone happy. The way you take care of him … frankly, I'm jealous."

The words sounded nice, and yet Ivy couldn't get over Scott's tone. She knew she was sensitive because of their previous encounter – and finding a dead body the night before – but there was something off about the way Scott looked at her. She didn't like it.

"You shouldn't be jealous," Ivy said. "You have a great wife. Maybe you should focus on her and worry less about Jack. We're happy and content."

"In case you haven't noticed, you're out here doing something active and fun and my wife is sitting by the campfire complaining with the other women," Scott pointed out. "You're a fun woman. I want a fun woman."

Ivy swallowed hard, reminding herself it was just an offhand comment and she shouldn't take personally. "Maybe you should try talking to Melissa about this."

"Melissa only cares about Melissa," Scott shot back. "I want someone who cares about me."

"Well, I hope things work out for you," Ivy said, climbing into her kayak and forcing a smile for Scott's benefit. "The man I care about needs help with learning how to kayak. I … ."

The sound of splashing assailed Ivy's ears, and when she swiveled she wasn't surprised to find Jack in the water as Donnie and Alex loudly guffawed a few feet away.

"I told you not to tip me over," Jack sputtered, wiping the water from his face. "Why didn't you listen to me?"

"What fun would that be?" Donnie challenged.

"Ivy!" Jack bellowed. "I need you to come out here and show my ... former friends ... what it means to be on your bad side."

"I'm coming," Ivy said, casting one more look in Scott's direction. "You need to stop living your life worrying about what other's have – what Jack has, for that matter – and focus on your own life.

"Jack is happy. *We're* happy," she continued. "Tearing others down isn't going to make you feel better. It's just going to make everyone else miserable, too."

Ivy shifted her attention to where Jack struggled to get back in his kayak. "I'm coming for you, Donnie," she warned. "If I were you, I'd start paddling now."

"I'm not afraid of no girl," Donnie scoffed, although his eyes shifted from happy to wary when he saw how fast Ivy was moving. "Holy crap! I guess Jack wasn't exaggerating when he said you could kayak."

"Go and get him," Jack ordered. "I'll give you whatever you want tonight if you dunk him."

"Oh, honey, the pleasure of dunking Donnie is the only reward I need," Ivy said.

"And you're still my favorite person ever," Jack said. "Kick him where it hurts ... and when he cries, show him no mercy."

Twelve

"They are just so … ." Maria broke off, her gaze fixed on Ivy and Jack as they sat under a tree about fifty feet away.

"Happy?" Scott supplied.

"I was going to say sickening," Maria replied. "What do you think their deal is?"

The six friends sat by the fire as the afternoon waned and dinner approached. Despite her ordeal the night before, Ivy seemed to be in good spirits as she sat on the ground facing Jack, her legs resting over his as he relaxed against a tree. Whatever they were saying to each other had them both laughing, and their fellow campers couldn't drag their eyes away from them.

"I think they're in their own little world," Donnie said. "They're kind of cute. I've never seen Jack smile this much."

"I think it has to be an act," Lauren interjected. "They're always touching each other and whispering … and no one needs to nap as often as they do."

"Oh, give them a break," Alex chided. "They're in that heady beginning portion of a relationship. Don't you guys remember what that was like? All you can do is think about the other person."

"Thankfully that goes away," Donnie teased, playfully poking Lauren's ribs.

"I don't think it's an act," Melissa offered. "We were with them at the museum yesterday, and whatever they've got going for them ... they both seem to enjoy it."

"I think it's temporary," Scott said. "Jack needed to be pulled out of his funk, and she came along at just the right time. There's no way he'll stay in Shadow Lake. It's tiny. Is he going to make her his entire world?"

"I would be very careful if I were you," Alex cautioned. "What you said to Ivy yesterday was out of line, and Jack is not going to put up with it if you say something stupid to her again."

"What did you say to her?" Melissa asked, turning her attention to Scott. "I knew something was wrong once we got to the restaurant, but no one would tell me what happened."

"Not everything I do is your concern," Scott shot back.

"He told Ivy we were all worried about Jack killing himself after the shooting," Alex supplied.

"Why would you do that?" Maria asked. "You were the only one who thought that. We were all worried about him being depressed, but I never thought he would kill himself."

"I thanked her for making him smile again," Scott clarified. "Don't go accusing me of things because she took it the wrong way."

"Jack took it that way, too," Alex pointed out. "I tried to smooth things over with him. I told him we were all worried and thrilled he found Ivy. Don't say anything like that to her again."

"That is awful," Melissa said, shaking her head. "Jack brought Ivy here because he wanted everyone to get to know her, not because he wanted you to scare her away."

"I think it was the other part of the conversation that bothered Jack more," Alex said, locking gazes with Scott. "Do you want to tell them what you said, or should I?"

"Oh, well, you're doing such a bang-up job of it, I would hate to take it way from you," Scott sneered.

"He also told Ivy that Jack was going to move away and she was essentially a fling," Alex said, not missing a beat. "He told her it wasn't a bad thing and she should feel good about herself."

Maria's mouth dropped open. "You cannot be serious?"

"What? We all know Jack is going to move back to the city once he gets his head in gear," Scott argued. "I thought Ivy should be aware of it in case she falls in love with him and gets her heart broken."

"I have news for you," Alex said, leaning forward. "Jack is never going back to the city. He's happy in Shadow Lake. He doesn't want to go back to the life he had before.

"Now, I don't know if this relationship is going to last, but my gut tells me it is," he continued. "Look at those two … ."

Everyone shifted their attention to the spot where Jack and Ivy shared a cookie – and occasional kisses – as they chatted about something only they cared about.

"That right there isn't just a new relationship," Alex said. "They've both fallen hard for one another. I don't see Jack ever walking away from her."

"I don't care if he walks away from her or not," Maria said. "It drives me crazy that she's so perfect. She makes the rest of us look bad. You never should've said something like that to her, though, Scott. That was just cruel."

"I thought she deserved all of the facts." Scott obstinately crossed his arms over his chest.

"Or you think she's hot and you wanted to see if she was open for offers," Melissa corrected. "You're not fooling anyone. You think she's pretty and you've been drooling over her since you met her. Your problem is that she only has eyes for Jack."

"Shut up, Melissa," Scott growled.

Instead of firing back a nasty retort, Melissa got to her feet and moved away from the group.

"Nice," Maria hissed. "Can't you do anything right?"

"Apparently not."

IVY AND JACK WERE IN THE MIDDLE OF AN INCREDIBLE DREAM – the duo lazily floating on a raft in the middle of the ocean, complete with fruity drinks, of course – when a terrified scream split the night air and jolted them awake.

Ivy bolted to a sitting position, scanning the darkness for signs of life, when everything came tumbling back to her.

"What is that?" Jack asked, rolling to his side so he could escape the sleeping bag.

"Someone is screaming," Ivy answered, feeling along the tent floor until she found her shorts. "Get dressed before you run outside, Jack. You'll traumatize people if they see you naked."

"I'm going to take that as a compliment," Jack mumbled, slipping into his own shorts and watching as Ivy tugged on her sports bra and tank top. It was inside out, but he didn't bother pointing that out.

"You stay close to me, honey," Jack warned. "If something has happened … ."

"I have no desire to wander away," Ivy said, pushing Jack through the flaps. "Don't worry about that."

"Where you're concerned, I'm always worried," Jack muttered, grabbing Ivy's hand so he could keep her close.

Once they exited the tent, they found everyone else moving toward the road on the other side of the campsite.

"Do you see anything?" Jack called out.

"We just heard a scream," Donnie replied, Lauren clutching his arm. "I … what should we do?"

"Stick together," Jack replied, leading Ivy toward his friends. "It could be something innocuous. Maybe kids are fooling around or something."

As if on cue, another scream hit the air. This one was blood-curdling enough to send chills down Ivy's spine. "That sounds like a child."

Jack glanced down at her. "You stay right with me."

Ivy didn't offer an answer other than squeezing his hand. They broke into a run, moving to the right where they both thought the noise originated from. When a third scream pierced the campground's quiet ambiance, they increased their pace until they found a group of people standing close to a dwindling campfire. They pulled up short, Jack approaching carefully so he didn't scare anyone.

"Is everyone okay?"

The group parted to look at him, several white faces offering stark expressions against the night sky.

"Who are you?" one of the men asked.

"My name is Jack Harker. I'm a police detective over in Shadow Lake. We heard the screams. Is everyone okay?"

The man pointed lower to the ground, causing Jack and Ivy to peer around a robust woman as she tried to control a hysterical child. "I think he had a nightmare."

"Is that all?" Jack asked, taking a step forward and fixing the small boy – he couldn't have been older than five – with a friendly look. "Did you have a nightmare, bud?"

The boy jerked away from the woman – Ivy assumed it was his mother – and shook his head so ferociously she was afraid it was going to roll off of his shoulders if he wasn't careful. "It wasn't a bad dream. I saw it!"

"What did you see?" Jack asked.

"It was a werewolf."

Jack shot a sidelong look at Ivy, his shoulders relaxing. "Did you put him up to this?"

"HE'S VERY IMAGINATIVE," SHANNON WEXLER SAID, RUNNING a hand through her hair as she watched her son stomp around the campsite ten minutes later. "I'm sorry he scared everyone, but he obviously didn't see anything."

"Yes, I did!" Hayden Wexler was a handful, and Ivy couldn't help but smile at the small boy as he paced a path around his mother. "I know what I saw."

"What did you see?" Jack asked, his eyes kind. "Did you see a shadow that looked like a werewolf?"

"No, I saw a real werewolf," Hayden shot back. "I know the difference between real and pretend, and this was real."

"Can you tell me what he looked like?" Ivy asked, sitting on the picnic table bench so she was closer to Hayden's level.

"He looked like a werewolf," Hayden replied.

"I know that, and I believe you," Ivy said. "There are different kinds of werewolves, though. Just like people, they have different colored hair and ... well ... sometimes they even wear clothes."

Jack pursed his lips as he watched her, his mind momentarily going to some future time where he could picture her talking that way to one of their children. It was a sobering – and nice – image. He quickly shook himself out of his reverie. They'd barely begun dating. Something like that was still a long way off. Still, he never pictured himself having children until Ivy came along. He filed the feelings away to study later and focused his attention on Hayden as the boy began to describe his monster.

"He had brownish yellow hair," Hayden said.

"Did it look dirty?"

"It looked like it smelled," Hayden answered, wrinkling his nose and making an adorable face.

"Was he tall?" Ivy asked, tilting her head to the side.

"Everybody is taller than me."

"Good point," Ivy said. "Was he tall like your mom?"

Hayden shook his head. "He was big like him." He pointed toward Jack. "He was scary like him, too."

Jack frowned. "Why do you think I'm scary?"

"Because you're a giant," Hayden replied, his eyes widening.

"Ah."

"What were you doing when you saw the werewolf?" Ivy asked.

"I was trying to hear what everyone was talking about."

"What do you mean?" Ivy asked.

"He was supposed to be in his tent sleeping because it's past his bedtime, but I think he was poking his head out of the tent and eaves-dropping," Shannon supplied.

"Where is his tent?" Jack asked.

Shannon pointed toward a small domed tent on the far side of the campsite. "We put the kids in that area because we knew we were going to be up later than them."

"Even though that's not fair," Hayden said, crossing his arms over his chest.

"You'll live," Shannon said.

"Not if the werewolf gets me!"

"There is no werewolf," Shannon snapped. "Knock it off."

"Nobody believes me," Hayden said, dejectedly kicking the ground.

"I believe you," Ivy said, patting his shoulder to get him to focus on her again. "Where did you see the werewolf?"

"He was standing over there," Hayden answered, pointing at the tree line. "I didn't see him at first, but then he moved and … I saw him." The last three words were barely a whisper.

"Did he look at you?"

Hayden nodded.

"Did he say anything?"

"He just looked at me," Hayden said. "I opened my mouth to yell for Mommy, but no sound would come out."

"Some sound came out," Jack pointed out.

"I had to try a couple of times."

"That's okay," Jack said. "You were brave in the face of danger and you protected everyone. We're very proud of you."

"I heard Mommy talking to Daddy, and they said there's some sort of animal out there that's eating people," Hayden said, his serious green eyes locked onto Ivy's face. "Do you think that's true?"

"I think that your mommy and daddy will keep you safe no matter what," Ivy replied, affectionately tousling his hair. "You did the right thing by yelling. You probably scared the werewolf away."

"What if he comes back?"

"He won't come back," Jack said. "Your mom and dad will make sure of that."

Shannon offered Ivy and Jack a wan smile and then gathered Hayden close. "I think it's time to put you to bed, little hero."

Hayden didn't look thrilled with the prospect. "Can I sleep with you tonight?"

"Just this once," Shannon said, giving in.

"What do you think?" Jack asked, moving to Ivy's side as the rest of Hayden's campsite compatriots dispersed so they could get some rest.

"I think he saw something," Ivy replied.

"The dogman?"

"I didn't say that," Ivy said. "Hayden is five. You heard him. To him you're a giant."

"He seemed to like you," Jack interjected.

"Kids always like me," Ivy said. "I think it's my hair."

"I think they sense you're a good person," Jack countered, slinging an arm over Ivy's shoulders and pressing a kiss to her forehead. "Kids can often see whether someone is good or bad before adults can."

"I think you're just whipped," Ivy teased.

"That, too," Jack agreed. "Do you think he saw a person and got scared?"

"Probably," Ivy said. "It's no different than me when I heard that dogman story as a kid and Max jumped out of the bushes to scare me. He probably saw someone walking and overreacted."

"If you believe that, why do you look so troubled?"

"Because I can't think of one reason anyone would be walking into the woods this late at night," Ivy answered. "A teenage girl was found mauled in there twenty-four hours ago. Knowing that, why would anyone risk going in there at this hour?"

"You have a very sharp mind, honey," Jack said, following her gaze. "You think like a cop sometimes."

"Is that a good thing?"

"Everything you do is good."

"I see you're bucking for a repeat nap under the stars," Ivy teased, letting Jack lead her back to their campsite.

"Actually, I'm perfectly happy cuddling up next to you and listening to you snore," Jack replied.

"I don't snore."

"You do when you sleep on your back," Jack countered. "Why do you think I always want you sleeping on my chest?"

"Because you like to cop a feel in your sleep."

"See, there's that mind again," Jack said. "You're always thinking."

"Where did your friends go?" Ivy asked, glancing around. While all six of them initially followed Jack and Ivy to the second campsite, she suddenly realized they were alone.

"They lost interest when Hayden announced it was a werewolf," Jack answered. "They're probably all asleep."

"That was ... nice of them."

"I'm glad they didn't hang around," Jack said. "I liked seeing you in action with Hayden. You were really good with him."

"I told you already, kids just seem to like me."

"They're not the only ones," Jack said. "Come on. Now a repeat nap is sounding like the perfect way to wear ourselves out so we can fall asleep. We'll be too keyed up otherwise."

"Well, as long as you have a practical reason, who am I to argue?"

Thirteen

"We're going fishing, honey," Jack announced the next morning, moving to Ivy's side as she cleaned up the breakfast remains.

Ivy arched an eyebrow. "Do you want me to congratulate you?"

Jack scowled. "I want to know if you want to come with us," he said. "I love fishing. You know that. We do it in our dreams all the time."

Ivy pressed her lips together and glanced around to see if anyone was listening. Apparently Jack and Ivy's conversation wasn't one for the record books. "Watch what you say," she whispered.

"I'm sorry," Jack said, his expression earnest. "I got used to being able to talk openly about that stuff around Max. I won't do it again."

"Thank you," Ivy said. "As to your question, though, no. I can't go fishing."

"Why not?"

"Because I can't kill an animal," Ivy replied, unintentionally shuddering. "I would feel guilty forever if I did that."

"We go fishing all the time when we're asleep," Jack pointed out, keeping his voice low. "You always pick bright pink lures to match your hair."

"Those aren't real fish," Ivy pointed out. "Even though those dreams feel real, in my mind I know I'm not really killing animals so I can play along and make you happy."

"I don't want to leave you here," Jack admitted.

"I'm fine," Ivy said, her eyes widening. "You do realize I entertained myself all the time before you came along, right?"

"I don't like to think about the dark times before we were together," Jack teased, pushing Ivy's hair away from her face and giving her a soft kiss before sobering. "I'm not worried about you entertaining yourself. I'm worried that you don't particularly seem to like the other women – and they're the only ones who will be here this afternoon."

"I like them fine," Ivy protested.

Jack lifted his eyebrows to almost comical heights.

"Fine," Ivy conceded. "I probably wouldn't choose to spend time with them on my own. I am determined to be nice to them because it's important to you, though, so you have nothing to worry about. I promise I won't pull anyone's hair or call them a nasty name."

"You are so adorable sometimes," Jack said, cupping the back of Ivy's head. "The thing is, I'm not particularly worried about you being mean to them. I'm worried about them trying to isolate you because … well … they're like chickens. They're likely to pick one outsider to peck to death."

"I had absolutely zero female friends growing up so I'm used to that."

"See, that just makes me sad," Jack said, pulling Ivy to him and hugging her. "I'll blow off fishing and we can go back to that Call of the Wild place. You never got to shop like you wanted the first time."

"We can go back to Call of the Wild whenever we want," Ivy reminded him. "It's less than an hour away from Shadow Lake. I think you should go fishing with your friends and have a good time."

"But … what are you going to do?"

"I'll probably go kayaking."

"Alone?"

"Jack." Ivy made a disgusted sound in the back of her throat.

"Fine, go kayaking." Jack gave in. "Please don't go too far out … and be careful. I will be inconsolable if something happens to you."

"You don't have to worry about that," Ivy said. "Didn't I prove to you yesterday that I'm queen of the kayak?"

"You're queen of everything," Jack said, giving Ivy another kiss before separating. "Wish me lots of fish. I'll be responsible for dinner tonight."

"That's good," Ivy said. "I won't eat fish and I certainly won't clean them."

"Wow, I finally found something you can't do," Jack teased. "I'm shocked."

"I didn't say I couldn't do it," Ivy argued. "I said I wouldn't do it."

"That's just semantics, honey," Jack said. "I still like you anyway. Don't worry."

IVY LASTED EXACTLY FIVE MINUTES AT THE CAMPSITE BEFORE SHE excused herself for the afternoon. Between Maria's constant complaining, Melissa's constant pouting, and Lauren's constant whining, she was at her wit's end. There was a reason Ivy never had female friends: She was convinced she didn't speak the same language.

When Ivy wanted to complain, she picked a fight and made sure the war she wanted to wage was worth winning. When Ivy wanted to pout ... well, she pouted. She just refused to do it for hours – and subsequently days – on end. A few hours of morose self-reflection was generally all Ivy could handle. As for whining, Ivy never considered herself to be much of a whiner. She would rather duke it out than prey on the pity of others.

Ivy was halfway to the main cabin when she decided to change course. As much as she wanted to kayak, she needed to check on something else first. She moved past the campsite from the night before, smiling and waving at Shannon as she headed toward the trees.

Ivy stepped lightly, studying the ground as she investigated the small parcel of land for clues. She was so intent on her task she almost jumped out of her skin when a small figure hunkered down next to her.

"Is that a werewolf print?" Hayden asked, awed. "I told you!"

"Hayden! Don't you dare wander away after last night," Shannon warned, grabbing her son's hand and giving him a dirty look. "You're in enough trouble as it is after freaking everyone out last night."

"Aw, Mom," Hayden complained. "I was just talking to Ivy. Look. She found the werewolf print."

"Did you really find a werewolf print?" Shannon asked, dubious.

"No," Ivy replied, her mind busy. "I did find a shoe print, though. Hayden, is this where you saw the werewolf?"

Hayden nodded. "I don't think werewolves wear shoes."

"No," Ivy agreed, patting him on top of his head. "People do, though. You listen to your mother and stay close to camp."

"What are you going to do?" Shannon asked.

"Follow the shoe print," Ivy replied. "I'm dying to see a werewolf live and in person."

Ivy wasn't an expert tracker by any stretch of the imagination, but she managed to follow the shoe print with relative ease as she walked through the woods. In the back of her mind she could hear Jack ranting and raving when he found out what she'd done, but she couldn't turn back now so she was going to have to live with the consequences of her decision. She saw a big fight in their future.

Ivy was initially worried the prints would lead to the clearing, and then she would have a hard choice in front of her. She didn't think she could return to that spot after seeing Kylie Bradford's body. Jack had promised to call the police to get an update on the case later that evening, but in her heart she knew that Kylie didn't accidentally fall and hit her head. Someone killed her and left her to be discovered. They created the macabre tableau for one reason: to get attention.

Ivy followed the footprints for almost twenty minutes before they disappeared into heavy growth. She took a deep breath and pushed through the dense line of trees, exhaling heavily when she found herself in an open expanse with a tiny shack in front of her. She glanced around, confused. She realized too late she wasn't alone.

"Are you lost?"

Ivy swiveled quickly, taking an inadvertent step back when she caught sight of the behemoth of a man standing behind her. Jack was tall, so she was used to looking up, but this man was … mammoth. His hair was blondish red and long, running into a wiry beard that hung low and was shot through with gray. His eyebrows were like spark plugs – the hair going in eighty different directions – and the look on his craggy face was cross.

"I ... um ... ."

"Well, speak up," the man said, looking Ivy up and down. "You don't look lost."

"I'm not lost," Ivy said, forcing her mind to calm as she debated her options. "You're the werewolf, aren't you?"

The man took Ivy by surprise when he chuckled. "That's a new one. Most people just call me by my name ... or 'hey you.' If you want to call me a werewolf, though, more power to you. If you're looking for the state campground, it's back that way about a mile."

"I thought this was state land," Ivy said.

"Most of it is," the man replied. "My family has owned this acreage for more than fifty years, though, and no matter how much those jerk-wads from the state bother me, I'm not selling it. They're going to have to wait until I die."

"My name is Ivy Morgan. I live over in Shadow Lake."

"Morgan, huh? Are you any relation to Michael Morgan?"

Ivy almost fell over she was so surprised. "He's my father," she said. "I ... how do you know my father?"

"I bought that bush over there at his nursery about two years ago."

Ivy scowled. "His nursery? That's my nursery."

"He said it was his," the man said. "I don't suppose it matters in the grand scheme of things. It's nothing to get your panties in a wad about."

"Don't talk about my panties," Ivy challenged.

"Why? Are you even wearing any? You don't look like the type of woman who bothers wearing them."

Ivy knit her eyebrows together, her previous fear shifting to the side to make room for irritation. "And you look like the type of man who hasn't seen panties in his entire life," she shot back. "How would you know?"

The man laughed, the sound a low rumble emanating from his belly. "You're funny. I'll give you that."

"What's your name?"

"Andrew Devlin," the man replied. "Tell your father I said hello when you see him again. You should probably get back to the campground if you know what's good for you. The police have been out here the last few days and something fishy is going on in these woods. You shouldn't be wandering around alone."

"I'm nowhere near done talking to you," Ivy said. "I know all about the body that was found. I'm the one who found it."

"Is that right?" Andrew asked, arching an eyebrow. It looked like a caterpillar was trying to escape from his forehead.

"Yes," Ivy said. "Were you at the campground last night?"

"What's it to you?"

"Did you look at a little boy in a tent?"

"Hey, I'm not some kind of weird pervert," Andrew snapped. "I don't go after little boys."

"That came out wrong," Ivy said, holding her hands up. "A little boy at one of the campsites claimed a werewolf was looking at him last night. I think he was talking about you."

"And why would you think that?"

"Because I followed the footprints you left in the dirt at the edge of the woods and they led me here."

"Ah, well ... I guess that explains why you came this far out," Andrew said, shaking his head. "I went over there to look around. The cops were making such a ruckus I wanted to see if I could hear anything. I didn't mean to scare that kid ... and I wasn't looking at him. I was standing off to the side and I saw him poke his head out. He looked at me and then he started yelling loud enough to wake the dead. I got out of there right quick."

"I figured he was confused," Ivy said. "I didn't know anyone lived out here."

"That's because I keep to myself and stay out of other people's business."

"Did you hear anything the night Kylie Bradford was killed? It would've been three nights ago."

"Listen, I like to keep to myself, but if I heard a girl screaming I would help," Andrew replied. "The police have already been here questioning me. I don't have anything to tell you or them."

"Do you think it was an animal?"

"I don't think there's an animal mean enough in these woods to do anything of the sort."

"I don't either," Ivy admitted. "I think someone at that campground killed her and then mutilated her in an effort to make it look like it was animals to cover his tracks."

"I think whoever did that might not have even cared if people thought it was animals," Andrew countered. "If someone is sick enough to carve up a teenage girl, he was probably proud of himself and wanted to show off his ... art."

Ivy made a face, although she couldn't argue with him. She'd been thinking the same thing herself. "Have you seen anyone strange running around these woods?"

"Just you."

"Well, I guess I should let you get back to ... whatever it is you do out here," Ivy said. "Try not to scare the kids again. You're too old to lurk. If you want to visit the campground, you're more than welcome to visit us."

"I don't like people," Andrew charged. "Why would I want to visit you?"

"I think you like people just fine," Ivy said. "I think what you're really worried about is that people won't like you."

"And what makes you think that?"

"Because I'm the same way."

Andrew's expression was thoughtful for a moment. Finally, he blew out a long-suffering sigh and gestured for her to follow him. "As long as you're out here, I have something to show you. I was going to call the police myself once I discovered it ... but I think you'll save me the trip to town to use the phone."

"You don't have a phone?"

"I have no one to call," Andrew said. "Come on. It's not very far away. I have a feeling you're going to want to see it anyway."

"You said you're not a pervert who goes after kids," Ivy said. "You're not a pervert who goes after women, are you?"

Andrew chuckled. "You're funny," he said. "You're safe with me. Trust me."

Ivy wasn't sure why, but she did trust him. "Just be aware, I bite and I hit if someone tries to back me into a corner."

"Well, I'm definitely looking forward to that," Andrew deadpanned.

Fourteen

"Where is everyone?" Jack asked, scanning the campsite for faces after returning from his fishing trip. The only person present was Melissa — and she didn't look happy.

"That's just what I was about to ask you," Melissa said, lifting a beer to her lips and slamming three large gulps.

"Don't you think it's a little early in the day for that?" Jack knew he sounded like a bossy jerk, but he hated seeing Melissa continuously wallow.

"Not really." Melissa didn't appear bothered by Jack's suggestion. "Where are the guys?"

"They walked up to the ranger cabin to get bags of ice."

"You mean they walked up to the ranger cabin so they could stay away from here a little while longer," Melissa corrected. "Don't worry. I'm well aware of how Scott feels about me. The last thing he wants to do is spend time with me if he can help it."

"You guys need to work out your own issues," Jack said. "I don't want to be a part of it."

"Of course not," Melissa shot back. "You're happy with your pink-haired girlfriend."

"Leave Ivy out of this, too."

"Why?"

"Because she hasn't done anything to you and it's not her fault that you're unhappy in your marriage," Jack replied. "I'm not joking with you, Melissa. I can see you're ticked off at the world. You might have a reason for it. You might not. I don't want to be a part of it, though."

Melissa staggered to her feet and took a step in Jack's direction, her legs unsteady. "Maybe you're the reason I'm so upset. Have you considered that?"

"I've barely talked to you since we got here." Jack was irritated. "Did you see where Ivy went?"

"She said something about getting a kayak," Melissa replied. "That was hours ago, though. You know what? She's probably out practicing her Wonder Woman routine. I can just see her leaping tall buildings in a single bound. She can do everything else. Why not that?"

"That's Superman," Jack clarified.

"What's Superman? Are you saying she's Superman?" Melissa was clearly drunk.

"No. I'm saying Superman leaps tall buildings in a single bound," Jack said. "Did Ivy say when she would be back?"

"Ivy doesn't really talk to me," Melissa answered. "We don't have a lot in common. I'm okay with that, though. I want to have a lot in common with you instead." Melissa ran her finger up Jack's chest, plastering what Jack was sure she believed to be a flirtatious look on her face. "Do you want to go into my tent with me and take a nap, Jack?"

Jack grabbed Melissa's finger and shoved it back in her direction. "No."

"Oh, what? Are you too good for me, Jack?"

"Yes." Jack was at his limit.

"So, you're fine with your pink-haired vixen, but a normal woman can't even compete. Is that what you're telling me, Jack?"

"You're drunk, Melissa," Jack said.

"I think Ivy must be magic," Melissa slurred, refusing to back down. "I know my husband wants to see her naked — although he already has. You're infatuated with her. I guess a regular woman can't compete."

"Melissa, as far as I'm concerned, no one can compete with Ivy," Jack snapped. "Now, what direction did she go in when she left?"

"I can't remember."

"Go and sleep it off, Melissa," Jack ordered. "You're embarrassing yourself." He turned to leave the campsite, intent on asking the ranger at the cabin when Ivy said she would return with the kayak, but his cell phone dinged with an incoming text message and distracted him.

He pulled the phone out of his pocket and scanned Ivy's message – which was long – and scowled. "I am definitely going to kill her this time."

"That would be great for us all," Melissa intoned, throwing herself in a chair and reaching for another beer. "Make sure you hide her body better than whoever killed that teenager did. You don't want to go to jail."

Melissa wasn't quite done talking to herself. "I don't know why we came back here after how badly last year's camping trip went," she lamented. "This place sucks."

"Sober up, Melissa," Jack snapped, stalking toward the woods. "If you're like this when I get back, we're going to have a problem."

"Have fun killing Ivy," Melissa sang to his back. She was lost in her own little world, and it was one Jack didn't want to visit.

JACK WASN'T SURE HE WAS IN THE RIGHT PLACE UNTIL HE SAW Ivy step out of the trees and lock gazes with him as he trudged down the campground's service road twenty minutes later. He broke into a run when he saw her, grabbing her shoulders when he got close enough to touch her and giving her a good shake.

"Are you trying to kill me?"

"Not last time I checked," Ivy replied dryly. "I'm sorry I had to text you, but you're going to want to see what Andrew discovered."

"Who is Andrew?"

"The werewolf."

"Ivy, I'm really close to losing it," Jack said. "You were supposed to be kayaking. I got back to camp and found Melissa soused. I have no idea where Maria and Lauren are. You were nowhere to be found. This is just ... unacceptable."

"I'm sorry, Jack," Ivy said, tugging on her limited patience and reminding herself that she knew this would happen when she opted to strike out on her own for the afternoon. "I stopped by the campsite from last night because I wanted to see if I could find any footprints close to the tree line.

"It was too dark to look last night," she continued. "Plus, the more I thought about it, I really did believe Hayden saw something that he couldn't wrap his mind around."

"A werewolf?"

"No," Ivy said, biting her tongue to keep herself from saying something truly terrible. "I followed the tracks to a shack. The owner's name is Andrew Devlin. His family has owned a parcel in the middle of all of this state land for fifty years."

"And you just wandered off with a stranger who might be a werewolf in his off time?" Jack wanted to shake her again. He wisely kept his hands to himself.

"He's not a werewolf."

"Thanks for the news tip."

"He does sort of look like Grizzly Adams, though," Ivy conceded. "He knows my father."

Jack stilled. That made him feel a little better about the situation, although he had no idea why. "Do you want to enlighten me on why we're out here?"

"Oh, right," Ivy said, shaking her head. "I was talking to Andrew and he mentioned that he had something he wanted to show me."

"It wasn't in his pants, was it?"

"You're starting to bug me, Jack," Ivy warned. "He took me about a mile away from his cabin. He found something when he was out fishing today."

"What?"

"I think I better show you," Ivy said, turning to move back into the woods. "You're going to have to walk for about ten minutes. I'm sorry, but I didn't know how else to direct you to where I was."

"That makes me feel better."

"I understand you're angry, Jack, and I don't blame you," Ivy said, keeping her gaze locked on the ground so she wouldn't trip. In truth, she was afraid to look at Jack. She had a feeling what type of emotions she would find crossing his handsome face if she did, and it wasn't something she could handle. "I promise I wasn't in any danger today."

"You lucked out, Ivy," Jack countered. "What would've happened if your friend the werewolf attacked you? How would I have found you?"

"He's actually a nice guy."

"I don't care!" Jack exploded. "You showed no regard for your own safety today, Ivy. You showed no regard for me either, for that matter."

Ivy slowed her pace and finally risked a glance at Jack. His cheeks were flushed with angry color and her heart sank when she grasped what he was really saying. "I didn't think of it that way."

"You never do," Jack snapped. "Dammit! This was supposed to be a fun week where we could kayak and cuddle next to a campfire. Instead you're wandering off into the woods and finding bodies, my friend's wife is hitting on me, and you're hanging out with potential murder suspects. This week officially sucks."

"Wait a second ... who hit on you?" Ivy was incensed.

"That's what you took away from what I just said to you?"

"I ... yes," Ivy admitted, her heart rolling. "Who hit on you?"

"Melissa is drunk as a skunk and she's feeling sorry for herself because she thinks Scott wants to bend you over the picnic table," Jack replied. "She decided she wanted to even the playing field."

"Did you ... ?" Ivy didn't finish the question. She already knew the answer. She didn't rein in her out-of-control mouth until it was too late, though.

"Did I what?" Jack pressed. "Did I cheat on you? Is that what you're asking me?"

Ivy's eyes filled with unbidden tears. She had no idea where they came from. She didn't consider herself a crier, but here she was getting emotional over something she knew Jack would never do. "No," Ivy answered, her voice small. "I was going to ask if you set her straight, but I already knew the answer so I cut myself off."

"Are you crying?"

"No." Ivy surreptitiously brushed away a solitary tear. "I'm sorry. I know you would never betray me. This has gotten out of hand, and it's all my fault."

"It *is* your fault," Jack agreed.

The couple lapsed into uncomfortable silence as Ivy led Jack farther into the forest. She racked her brain for ways to make up with him, but she feared she'd gone too far this time and he was finally going to walk away when she showed him what Andrew found. To her surprise, Jack reached over and mutely snagged her hand about five minutes after they ceased talking, linking his fingers with hers as they continued to hike toward what Ivy was convinced would spell certain doom for their relationship.

"I thought you were angry with me?"

Ivy's voice was so sad it caused Jack's heart to roll. "I am angry with you," he said. "I don't want you to think something bad is going to happen because we're fighting, though. I know where your head keeps going, and I figure the only way to drum that out of you is to show you that I meant what I said when I promised I wouldn't leave."

"But ... you're about to be really furious with me."

"That doesn't mean I'm going to walk away."

"Are you sure? I think I might deserve it after today," Ivy said. "I didn't think about what I was doing. Actually, that's not true. I knew you would be angry. I still did it."

"I know."

"I'm sorry, Jack. I really am."

"I know you're sorry," Jack said. "I shouldn't have yelled at you the way I did. It's not fair. I knew when we started dating that you had a mind of your own. That's one of the things I like most about you.

"I need you to think before you do things," he continued. "You've already done this. We can't go back in time and fix it. We have to move forward. I don't want you crying, and I definitely don't want to keep yelling."

"You're going to yell when you see what Andrew found," Ivy interjected.

"Well, we'll deal with that when it happens," Jack said. "How close are we?"

"Close," Ivy replied. "It's right over here."

Ivy led Jack through a thick crop of trees and into a meadow, smiling in greeting when Andrew swiveled in their direction.

"I see he found you," Andrew said.

"He always does," Ivy said. "Andrew Devlin, this is Jack Harker."

"It's nice to meet you," Jack said, his manners ever-present as he shook the stranger's hand.

"The pleasure is all mine," Andrew deadpanned.

"Now is not the time to be crotchety," Ivy warned. "There's no reason to be a jackhole."

Andrew chuckled. "I really like you. You make me laugh."

"She definitely has a way about her," Jack agreed. "Show me what you found."

"It's right over here," Andrew said, leading Jack toward a small grouping of rocks at the far side of the clearing. "I almost didn't see it when I was walking past today, but for some reason I thought it looked weird so I decided to check it out."

"Jack, wait," Ivy said, pulling up short and tugging on his hand.

"What?"

Ivy threw her arms around his neck and hugged him. Jack was initially reticent, but he ultimately gave in and returned the embrace.

"What was that for?" Jack asked when they separated.

"I just wanted to make sure I got to touch you one last time."

"Don't get melodramatic, Ivy," Jack said. "Nothing is changing in our relationship no matter what you're about to show me. Well, that's not entirely true. I'm going to cuff you to me for the rest of this trip when we get back to camp, but other than that everything is going to be fine."

"You haven't seen what I want to show you yet," Ivy said.

Jack moved to Andrew's side and glanced down at the spot the grizzled man pointed toward, frowning when he realized what he was looking at. It was a human skull. It was almost completely covered with grass and errant flowers, but the telltale empty eye-sockets knocked Jack for a loop as they stared back at him.

"I was going to drive to town and call the police this afternoon,"

Andrew explained. "That's when I ran into your friend and I figured you two could help with this situation."

"Oh, Ivy," Jack muttered. "This is so bad."

"Are you going to break up with me now?"

"No," Jack answered. "I am worried the state police are going to lock you up and I'm only going to see you through a prison window for the next twenty years, though."

"What should we do?"

"I suggest praying," Andrew said.

"I suggest ... crap," Jack muttered. "This is absolutely going to bite."

Fifteen

By the time Ivy and Jack made it back to the campground, they both felt as if they'd been through the wringer. Twice. This time State Trooper Tad Harvey was nothing less than beastly when he questioned Ivy about how she managed to discover a body in the middle of nowhere. No matter how angry he was with her, that got Jack's hackles up and the two men almost came to blows in the middle of a crime scene.

Five curious faces landed on the couple as they trudged into the campsite shortly after dark. Jack was relieved to see Melissa wasn't present, which hopefully meant she'd passed out while he was gone. That was the last thing he wanted to deal with.

"What happened to you two?" Donnie asked, his eyes wide. "Did you guys go native in the woods?"

"We've been dealing with the state police," Jack replied, rolling his neck until it cracked and directing Ivy toward the open chairs on the far side of the campfire.

"Do you want me to cook you dinner?" Ivy asked. She sounded as weary as Jack felt.

"I'm okay, honey," he said, snagging her around the waist and dumping her on his lap when she moved to sit in a separate chair. He wanted her close.

"Why were you dealing with the state police?" Scott asked. "Where did you even go?"

"Yeah, when we got back to the campsite with the ice, we found Melissa zonked out by the fire and everyone else gone," Alex said. "Maria and Lauren walked down to the boat launch to look around, but we had no idea where you and Ivy took off to."

"Ivy decided she wanted to find the werewolf from last night, so she followed a set of footprints close to that other campsite until she found a shack in the middle of the woods," Jack replied.

"That doesn't sound like a good idea to me," Maria chimed in.

"Yes, well, we're over that now," Jack said. "She found the were-wolf, by the way. It's a really crabby guy named Andrew Devlin. He looks like Santa Claus on steroids. He asked Ivy to go for a walk in the woods because he wanted to show her something, and she decided to go."

Ivy pressed her lips together to make sure she didn't say anything that might set Jack off again. He was exhausted, and the last thing she wanted to do was push him over the edge. That didn't mean she liked the way he was talking about her, but she wasn't willing to turn it into an argument.

"He wasn't a pervert, was he?" Scott asked.

Jack narrowed his eyes. He didn't like how Scott instantly jumped to that conclusion. "No. He was an old grump. He wasn't a pervert, though."

"What did he show you?" Lauren asked.

"A body."

The group fell silent for a moment, stunned disbelief washing over the collective gathering. Then everyone started talking at once.

"Are you serious?"

"Who was it?"

"How did they die? Was it another animal attack?"

"Was it another teenage girl?"

"Is this guy Ivy found a suspect?"

Jack blew out a frustrated sigh. "Um ... that's a lot of questions all at once," he said. "The body was older. It was actually just a skeleton. Some of the bones weren't there, and the state police guys believe scavengers carried them off. We might never know a cause of death.

"We don't know if it was a man or a woman right now, and we probably won't find out until tomorrow," he continued. "Ivy and I have to go to the state police outpost and answer more questions first thing in the morning. They cut us loose tonight because they need more information before they move forward."

"They can't honestly consider the two of you suspects," Alex scoffed. "You said yourself the body has been there for a long time. They'll probably never figure out who it is, let alone what happened."

"I don't think they legitimately consider us suspects," Jack said. "I do think Ivy discovering two bodies in one week makes things ... difficult."

"I'm sorry," Ivy murmured.

"I know," Jack said, brushing her hair away from her face and pressing a soft kiss to her cheek. "It's okay."

"What about this guy you found in the woods?" Lauren asked. "Do you think he could be a suspect?"

"I think he's happy being left to his own devices and he has no motive for killing anyone," Jack replied.

"You don't know that," Alex pressed. "He could be a deviant. You spent two hours with the guy."

"If he was a deviant and responsible for a murder, he wouldn't have volunteered to take Ivy to the scene and not touch her," Jack said. "He's harmless. He seems like a good guy, although his social skills leave a little bit to be desired. He's not a killer."

"If you say so," Alex muttered.

"What do you think the police want to talk to you guys about tomorrow?" Donnie asked.

"I think they want to see if our stories change," Jack answered. "I also think they'll be placing calls to my partner and anyone else in Shadow Lake who might have dirt on us before we even get there."

"What happens if they try to arrest you?" Maria asked.

"They can't arrest us," Jack replied. "We haven't done anything, and they have absolutely nothing on us but suspicion."

"I hope you're right," Donnie said. "That would be a bummer ending for our camping trip."

"It will be fine," Jack said, resting his chin on Ivy's shoulder for a moment.

"I'm really tired," Ivy said.

"I am, too," Jack said. "Let's go to bed. After what you've put me through today, I deserve a long massage."

"I think you've definitely earned it."

AFTER SAYING GOODNIGHT TO EVERYONE, JACK AND IVY retired to their tent and wordlessly stripped out of their clothes. Ivy climbed into a pair of cotton shorts and a tank top, while Jack settled for his boxer shorts.

"Are you okay, Ivy?"

Ivy lifted her eyes and forced a weak smile. "I'm fine. Are you okay?"

"Come here a second," Jack said, patting the spot between his legs as he settled on the sleeping bags. Ivy crawled to him, snuggling close as he wrapped his arms around her and kissed her cheek. "I know you're upset. I don't want to start another argument, but we need to talk for a second."

"I thought you wanted a massage."

"I thought I did, too," Jack admitted. "It turns out what I really want is to crawl into this sleeping bag and go to sleep. I am mentally and physically exhausted, and I think you're probably worse off than I am. That doesn't mean we're going to bed without talking this through."

"Are you going to yell?"

"No."

"Do you want to yell?"

Jack chuckled. He couldn't help himself. "I would be lying if I said I didn't enjoy fighting with you," he said. "I prefer fighting over little things, though. This is a big thing."

"I've been taking care of myself for a long time," Ivy said, licking her lips. "Calling someone to ask permission to do something doesn't come naturally to me."

"I don't want you to ask permission," Jack clarified. "I want you to be who you are without killing me with worry in the process. Trouble seems to find you, honey. I don't know why, but it does.

"I don't want to boss you around, no matter what you might think to the contrary. I also don't see myself as some sort of king who gets to rule you," he continued. "I do see myself as a man who would be extremely upset if something happened to you."

"I know."

"Ivy, what would you have done if you found something dangerous in the woods today?"

"I don't know," Ivy replied. "I'm sure I would've figured it out."

"How?"

Ivy shrugged. "I can't answer that without a specific scenario."

"Okay, what if you found out that Andrew was a murderer and he tried to grab you?"

"I would've kicked him in the nuts and ran into the woods so I could hide."

"The woods that he knows better than you?" Jack prodded.

"I know you have a point, and I can't rebut anything you're suggesting," Ivy said. "I don't have an excuse for what I did. It wasn't smart. I really am sorry."

"I don't want you to keep repeating that, and I really need you to stop worrying about infuriating me to the point where I'm going to leave you," Jack said. "We're in this together right now. I don't just mean this camping trip either.

"I knew the second I saw you that you were going to change my life," he continued. "I'm not sure how I knew it. I'm not sure if you felt what I was feeling. There was just something inside of me that couldn't let go of the idea of you."

"I felt something, too."

"I'm glad," Jack said. "I would hate to go out on this emotional limb on my own. I don't want you to stop being you. Just ... think before you do things."

"Should I ask myself 'what would Jack do'?" Ivy teased.

"That's exactly what I want you to start doing," Jack replied, tickling Ivy's ribs and flipping her so she was on her back on top of the sleeping bags. He lowered himself on top of her and kissed the tip of her nose. "Now, you're going to owe me the world's longest massage when we get home. I want you to do it right, though. I want those lotions you have all over your house to be used because I love the smell of them."

"I promise to massage you until you cry."

"No more crying, Ivy," Jack said. "I don't like it when you cry. As for that Melissa thing today, I don't know if you should say anything to her tomorrow. She was so drunk I have doubts she's going to remember what she did."

"Yes, but now that I ask myself 'what would Jack do' before I make any decisions, I have to say that I think you would say something if the situation was reversed," Ivy countered. "If someone hit on me – drunk or not – you would not take it lying down."

Jack ran his tongue over his teeth, conflicted. "You have a point."

"I always have a point."

"Not always, little missy," Jack said, mock growling as he kissed her neck. "If you want to say something to Melissa, I think you've earned it. From where I'm standing, though, you should know she's a very unhappy woman."

"I noticed that before you did."

"Let's not get into a 'who is smarter than who' contest, okay?"

"Fine," Ivy said, blowing out a frustrated sigh. "I understand what you're saying about Melissa. She seems to be genuinely miserable. Her husband is a jackass, too. I still don't like her hitting on you. You're mine."

"Oh, now who is being possessive?"

"I won't say anything as long as she doesn't do it again," Ivy said, giving in. "I hope you know that these people are really starting to bug me, though. I know they're your friends, but I just can't picture you spending a lot of time with them."

"College was a long time ago, honey," Jack said. "People change a lot in their twenties. I would like to remain friendly with the guys, but it's not like I see them being a big part of my future. It's more like they're going to be an occasional part of my past that visits once a year."

"Do you see me being a big part of your future?"

"Are you fishing for compliments?" Jack challenged.

"I'm asking an honest question."

"Ivy, when I look at you, all I see is our future," Jack said. "I know we haven't been dating long, and I know I fought getting together, but I can't imagine being without you. The thought makes me feel ill."

"That was a really good answer, Jack."

"I'm full of good answers."

"Why don't you pick the spot for us to dream tonight, and as soon as we're together, I'll show you what I think of that answer."

"Sold," Jack said, offering Ivy a scorching kiss before separating so they could crawl inside the sleeping bags. "Do you want a daytime or nighttime setting?"

Ivy killed the lantern and then rolled to her side, resting her head against Jack's chest as he tugged her close. "Surprise me."

Sixteen

"Thank you for agreeing to come in."

Trooper Tad Harvey looked liked he'd seen better days. His eyes were ringed with red, and pooling dark bags made him appear as if he hadn't slept in days.

"We want to help," Jack said, settling in one of the chairs across from Harvey's desk as Ivy took the other. "I'm a police officer. I know how this works. You have to question Ivy until you can rule her out."

"You, too."

"Me, too," Jack conceded.

"That's not fair," Ivy protested. "Jack wasn't even with me when I found either body."

"That's what *you* claim," Harvey countered. "I can't take your word for it. That's not how a proper investigation is conducted. I'm sure your boyfriend can explain that to you if you're confused."

"Oh, no," Ivy said. "I would much rather you keep talking to me in that tone so I can imagine I'm twelve again and roll my eyes like I did when my father used to lecture me about staying up past my bedtime."

Jack pursed his lips to keep from laughing, Ivy's tone warming his heart even though Harvey appeared ready to strangle her. He was worried about how defeated she was yesterday, but she was back to her chipper – and feisty – self today.

"Do you think that's funny?" Harvey asked.

"Not particularly," Ivy replied. "You don't look like you laugh a lot, though, so I won't take it personally that you're not laughing now."

"Calm down, tiger," Jack chided, reaching over to rest his hand on top of Ivy's. "Trooper Harvey has a job to do. Let's just answer his questions and get out of here. If you behave yourself I'll take you back to that Mexican restaurant you like for lunch so you can enjoy it this time."

Ivy sighed. "Fine. What do you want to know?"

"I want to know about you, Ms. Morgan," Harvey answered. "I placed a call to Shadow Lake this morning. I talked to a Detective Nixon because I wanted to ask him about his partner. He had a lot to say about you, too."

That was a trap. Ivy knew it. Brian Nixon would never say anything bad about her. He'd known her since she was a child. He'd coached Max on three different teams. He visited her house for summer barbecues at least once a month when the weather was warm. Harvey was fishing, and both Ivy and Jack knew it.

"Oh, yeah? What did Detective Nixon say?" Ivy's voice was unnaturally upbeat.

"He said that you had a tendency to find trouble," Harvey replied.

"No, he didn't."

"Yes, he did."

"No, he didn't," Jack chimed in. "Brian Nixon is my partner, and he loves Ivy. He's been friendly with her family for years. In fact, when we have a fight, he takes her side. He didn't say one bad thing about her, so stop trying to pretend he did."

Harvey scowled. "I guess I shouldn't be surprised at that," he said. "Shadow Lake is the size of a pinprick. Everyone there knows each other."

"I knew you would call Brian, so I'm not surprised that was the first thing you did this morning," Jack said. "I don't have a problem with it. We're not killers."

"I don't think you're killers either," Harvey conceded. "It's just …

you have to admit that Ms. Morgan stumbling across two different bodies in three days is highly suspect."

"I think it's a hard coincidence to swallow, but that's all it is," Jack said. "Ivy has no motive. Why would she kill a teenage girl? Why would she kill whoever that was we found in the woods yesterday?"

"Hannah Gibson," Harvey supplied. "That's the name of the girl Ms. Morgan found yesterday."

"You identified her fast," Jack commented. "How did you manage that?"

"It wasn't hard," Harvey replied. "Hannah went missing from the same campground almost exactly one year ago. She was there with her parents and disappeared in the middle of the night."

"Just like Kylie Bradford," Ivy said.

Harvey nodded. "The similarities have not escaped me," he said. "The problem we have is that the campground is a transient community. The only people who are there from year to year are the rangers."

"Have you started looking at backgrounds?" Jack asked.

"We have," Harvey answered. "We have no red flags at this time, and three overlapping workers. We're going to continue down that route, but it's not looking likely that any of those men could be killers."

"Well, if you look at it pragmatically, these cases might not be linked," Jack pointed out. "A year is a long cool down period."

"What's a cool down period?" Ivy asked.

"If we're to believe that both Hannah and Kylie were killed by the same person, that would suggest a serial killer," Jack explained. "Most serial killers ramp up their timetable as they go along. A year is a long time between kills."

"Only if he's just killing here," Ivy argued. "What if it's someone who comes camping at the park every year around the same time? He could be killing somewhere else, too."

"That's a pretty interesting theory," Harvey said. "I had it as well. The problem we have is that the coroner is still trying to ascertain a cause of death for Kylie Bradford. There was a lot of damage to her body, and many of her organs were missing."

"Do you think someone took them as trophies?" Jack asked.

"Probably not."

"So, what happened to them?"

"Animals took them first," Ivy answered for Harvey. "It's common for them to go for organs before flesh and then come back for the flesh. We're probably talking about several scavengers going after her body."

"How do you know that?" Jack asked, impressed.

"Max watches a lot of *Dateline* shows and I saw it on an episode about a woman who was dumped in the woods by her husband," Ivy answered.

"I'm going to start limiting your television time," Jack said.

"She's right," Harvey interjected. "We've talked to several animal experts, and all of them said the exact same thing she just did. There were no indentations on Kylie's skull, and that would seem to indicate she didn't suffer a head wound from a fall."

"Is the coroner declaring it murder?"

"He's calling it suspicious right now, but we're obviously leaning toward murder," Harvey replied. "We've pulled all of the campground records for the past two years. The good news is that people have to register at these state campgrounds ... and they have to present identification when they do."

"That's a lucky break," Jack said. "Do you have any names that appear both years?"

"We have six."

Jack's eyebrows shot up his forehead. "Seriously? I didn't realize people were so sentimental when it came to camping."

"A lot of people pick the same weekend to visit a campground from year to year," Harvey said. "That usually happens on holiday weekends, though. As you know, this isn't a holiday weekend."

"What have you found out about the returnees?"

Harvey licked his lips, his gaze bouncing between Ivy and Jack as he decided how to answer.

"It's not like we're going to tell anyone," Ivy prodded. "What's the problem?"

"The repeat names all happen to be sharing a campsite with you," Harvey answered.

"ARE YOU OKAY?" IVY ASKED AN HOUR LATER, DIPPING A tortilla chip in La Señorita's green salsa and studying Jack with compassionate eyes.

"I don't know what to think about this," Jack admitted, leaning back in the booth and shaking his head. "If Harvey is right, that means one of my friends could be a murderer."

"It could be a coincidence."

"Really? What are the odds?"

"What are the odds that I would stumble across two bodies in a matter of days and have nothing to do with either death?" Ivy challenged. "You don't have a problem believing in me. Why do you have such a problem believing in people you've known for ten years?"

"I don't know them like I know you," Jack answered. "I feel like I've known you my whole life. That's how comfortable I am with you. I used to know these guys, but time creates distance and people grow a lot when they're apart."

"I'm assuming you want to rule out Maria, Melissa, and Lauren for the time being," Ivy suggested. "If you look at Scott, Donnie, and Alex, does one of them jump out at you?"

"Not really. What about you?"

"Me?" Ivy was surprised by the question. "I barely know them."

"That makes your insight doubly important," Jack said. "You can look at my friends without seeing history and letting it cloud your opinion. Tell me what you think when you look at them. Don't try to spare my feelings."

"I think Alex is a thinker," Ivy said, not missing a beat. "He sits back and lets the others say stupid things because he wants to be the smartest guy in the room. I have no idea if he is, but he likes to think he is."

"He was definitely the smartest out of all of us in college," Jack confirmed. "It seemed easy for him, although he did study quite a bit when necessary. What else have you got?"

"Donnie is the class clown," Ivy said. "He's the least attractive of your group and he gets his attention by making jokes. He likes that attention, but he's really insecure. He wants you guys to look at him as an equal, but you're the only one who does. Alex talks down to him and Scott largely ignores him unless he wants to embarrass him."

"Wow," Jack muttered. "That was pretty insightful, honey. What about Scott?"

"I worry that I might be predisposed to dislike Scott because of what happened at Call of the Wild," Ivy admitted.

"I'll take that under consideration," Jack said. "Go ahead."

"Scott is a very unhappy individual," Ivy said. "So is his wife, although none of your friends seem particularly happy. I can dissect the women when we're done if you're so inclined."

"Let's stick with the men for now," Jack said, chuckling at Ivy's enthusiasm. He valued her opinion, and she appreciated that. He was happy letting her expound on his friends so he could think about what she suggested from a clinical perspective.

"Scott is a man who thought he was going to get everything he wanted because he made a life list," Ivy said.

"What's a life list?"

"It's when you mark milestones on a to-do list and set life goals accordingly," Ivy answered. "For example, Scott strikes me as a guy who needed to find a job within a month of graduation. He probably fooled around with a bevy of women until he was twenty-five and then married the one he was dating when he hit the age he thought he should be when he settled down. It didn't matter who she was, and now that's coming back to bite him.

"He probably had dates set for when he should get promoted ... and when he should buy his first house ... and when he should earn his first performance award," she continued. "He probably hit some of those goals. He probably missed others, though, and the ones he missed weigh on him."

"Scott has always liked a list," Jack mused.

"He's at a crossroad in his life," Ivy explained. "His marriage isn't working, and that means he'll probably have to sell his house in a divorce. If he's tense, maybe his work production has suffered and he's missed out on a promotion somewhere."

"You think it's him, don't you?"

Ivy shrugged. "I can't answer that," she said. "Under the right circumstances, I honestly think it could be any of them. The thing we need to remember is that it might be none of them, and you can't go barreling into camp tonight and bombard them with questions."

"What do you suggest I do?"

"Profile them when they're not looking," Ivy replied. "They can't suspect that you're feeling them out, because if they do you'll lose three friendships forever, and odds are only one of them is guilty."

"You're a smart woman, Ivy Morgan."

"And now you owe me a massage."

Seventeen

"Has anyone ever told you that you have a suspicious face?"

Ivy sidled up to Jack later that evening, making a show of wrapping her arms around his waist and resting her head against his chest so no one would suspect them of doing anything other than canoodling.

Jack aimlessly rubbed his hand up and down Ivy's back and chuckled. "Are you saying that I'm being too obvious?"

"I'm saying that you're standing in a corner staring at your friends and how they interact and it's becoming obvious that you're either angry about something, or suspicious."

Jack shifted his eyes to Ivy and tightened his arm around her back. "What do you want me to do? Shall we get drunk and play Spin the Bottle so I can spy amid distraction?"

"Only if you plan on limiting yourself to kissing dudes," Ivy replied, not missing a beat. "I'll have to smack you around if you kiss any of those women."

"I guess it's lucky that I only want to kiss you," Jack said, dropping a sweet kiss on her lips.

"I guess so," Ivy agreed, shifting so she could watch the people around the fire. They seemed oblivious to Jack and Ivy's solitude, but she knew looks could be deceiving. "I have an idea, if you're up for it, that is."

"I think a nap sounds great."

"Not that," Ivy chided, pinching his flank and causing Jack to squirm.

"You're vicious when you want to be."

"I'm just trying to get your attention."

"You'll never have a problem getting that, honey," Jack said. "What's your idea?"

"Just ... come with me to the fire," Ivy prodded. "We'll have a good cuddle and let me handle the talking. When we're done, I'll give you a short preview of your homecoming massage."

"You're not taking any time off of my massage," Jack argued.

"This is a bonus."

"You had me at cuddle," Jack whispered, smirking when he realized exactly what he'd said. "And there's something I never thought I would hear myself say."

"Don't worry. Your secret is safe with me."

Ivy and Jack joined the rest of the group, Ivy sitting on Jack's lap and tugging a blanket over them. They decided to listen to a few minutes of conversation before interjecting their own thoughts.

"I'll bet it was a bear," Maria said. "I saw a horror movie once, and there was a bear in it that stalked campers and ate them."

"Bears don't eat humans," Ivy corrected, internally chastising herself when she realized how overbearing she sounded. "They try to avoid humans most of the time."

"That's not what that movie said," Maria challenged.

"Did you see it on the SyFy channel?"

"So what?" Maria shot back. "That doesn't mean it's not real."

Ivy risked a glance at Jack and found him laughing into her shoulder. "This isn't funny," she whispered.

"You just have such a way with people, honey," Jack said, enjoying himself for the first time in hours. Now that he was looking at his friends with a critical eye – suspicions that one of them might be a murderer plaguing him – he saw Ivy as his only true ally.

"If it wasn't a bear, what was it?" Maria challenged.

"I think it was a person," Ivy replied, lacing her fingers with Jack's under the blanket and resting them on top of her stomach.

"How can you know that?" Scott asked. "Did the police tell you anything when you went to visit them this morning?"

"The trooper didn't really tell us a lot," Ivy said, her face taking on a faux concerned look that floored Jack. She was playing a part – and she was doing it masterfully because his friends didn't know her well enough to see what she was doing. "He mostly wanted to clear us so he could move on with his investigation."

"Is that normal?" Donnie asked.

"It is," Jack confirmed. "Ivy was never really a suspect, but he still had to rule her out. Finding both bodies was cause for concern, but he was happy to be able to cross her off his list."

"Does that mean they're looking for one suspect in both deaths?" Alex asked.

"They are," Ivy confirmed, taking Jack by surprise. "The trooper believes that both bodies are the work of the same individual."

Jack surreptitiously shifted under Ivy but remained quiet.

"How does that work?" Lauren asked. "Does that mean the killer is a local?"

"I'll bet it's that guy Ivy met in the woods," Donnie said. "Who else would it be?"

"They have a list of potential suspects, although they didn't share it with us," Ivy said. "I guess there are a few names on it."

"But ... how?" Scott asked. "How could they possibly tie two teenage girls together when they disappeared a year apart?"

Jack cleared his throat. "Who said it was two teenage girls?"

"I ... just assumed," Scott replied. "If they're looking for one killer in two deaths, it would stand to reason that the victims had something in common."

"We don't know anything about the second victim yet," Ivy lied. "We don't know if the body belongs to a male or female. I'm not sure if the state police know who it belongs to yet either."

"What are you doing?" Jack murmured so only Ivy could hear. She couldn't risk answering when they had an audience, so she remained impassive and watched his friends for reactions.

"I think it's creepy," Melissa said. She'd spent most of the evening avoiding eye contact with Jack, and she'd appeared mortified the two times she locked gazes with Ivy. "That could mean there's a serial killer out here."

"I'm guessing the troopers are checking all of the rangers first," Ivy volunteered. "The trooper we dealt with didn't want to share information – he thought I had attitude – but he did let it slip that they were gathering the names of campground guests to check against previous lists."

"What does that mean?" Scott asked.

"It means that this park is run by the state," Jack answered for Ivy. "Everyone shows their identification when they check in. The state records that in a database."

"I didn't know that," Maria said. "That's kind of invasive."

Jack shrugged. "I think it's going to turn out to be a good thing for investigators on this one."

"I agree," Ivy chimed in. "I mean ... how many people came to this exact campground two years in a row? It shouldn't take the troopers long to narrow down their list of suspects. After that? I'm guessing we'll see an arrest any day now."

"THAT WAS PRETTY INTERESTING," JACK SAID A HALF HOUR later as he walked with Ivy toward the ranger cabin. "You set them all up, lied when necessary, and then knocked them down with pertinent information that could make the guilty party panic. I'm impressed."

"I don't think you should be surprised that I'm a genius," Ivy said. "You should've known that from our first meeting."

"You mean the one where you insulted me and gave me dirty looks every chance you got?"

"I mean the one where I knew there was a body in the ditch and you didn't," Ivy corrected.

"If you weren't so cute, I'd spank your bottom blue for bringing that story up time and time again," Jack warned.

"That sounds kinky," Ivy replied, unruffled. "Just so you know, I'm not into that bondage and domination stuff … unless I'm the one dominating."

"Oh, see, now I'm turned on," Jack teased, easing his arm around Ivy's waist as they walked. "Do you want to tell me what we're doing out here? I thought the whole point of tonight was sitting back and watching my friends so we could figure out which one of them was a murderer."

"I'm worried you're fixating on your friends to the detriment of everyone else," Ivy said. "Listen, I know how it looks. That doesn't mean one of them is definitely a killer. I know you. You're going to feel guilty about your suspicions if it turns out none of them is a killer."

"You might be right," Jack conceded. "That still doesn't explain what we're doing out here."

"Well, I wanted to give them time to talk amongst themselves without worrying we were watching over them," Ivy replied. "They need to relax and give serious thought to the crumbs we dropped."

"That's sensible. How come I don't think that's the only thing on your mind?"

"Because you're coming to the realization – rather late, mind you – that I'm a genius," Ivy supplied. "I also want you to call Brian."

"Why? He has no jurisdiction here."

"No, but he can run background checks on all of your friends and get us information about unsolved homicides – or missing teenage girls – close to where they live," Ivy said. "Just because they might not be killers, that doesn't mean I want to overlook the fact that one of them could possibly be a very sick individual."

"You are a marvel, honey," Jack said, grabbing the front of her shirt and hauling her up to give her a smoldering kiss. "That's a great idea. Brian will be able to get us the information that Trooper Harvey doesn't want to share."

"There's no guarantee that we're going to find something," Ivy reminded Jack. "I don't want to miss anything either. I'm worried that someone is going to panic now that he thinks the police could be zeroing in on him."

"I need you to promise me that you're not going to wander around alone again for the rest of this trip," Jack said, his eyes serious. "I don't want to infringe on your freedom, but I need to know you're safe so I don't get distracted."

"I promise to stick close," Ivy said. "That's going to make going to the bathroom in the middle of the night difficult, though. I'm not sure we're ready for that much togetherness."

Jack snorted. "You're so cute."

"I'm waiting for you to solve that dilemma," Ivy prodded, crossing her arms over her chest.

"You're just going to have to go to the bathroom before we go back to our tent and not drink anything until morning."

"So you're going to torture me to keep me safe?"

"If that's the way you want to look at it," Jack replied, not missing a beat. "I'm going to keep you safe no matter what. You're going to have to get used to my protective instincts and deal with them."

"I guess I can live with that," Ivy sighed. "You're probably going to have to massage me to take my mind off of my bladder problems tonight."

"As long as you're naked, I'm fine with that."

"Oh, the compromises I make for you."

"I promise it will be worth it," Jack said, pulling his phone out of his pocket. "Part of me hopes we're wrong about this."

"All of me hopes we're wrong about this," Ivy said. "We have to be smart, though. I'm sorry."

"I'm sorry, too," Jack said. "No matter what, I don't think these friendships are going to survive this camping trip."

IVY'S MIND WAS MUDDLED WHEN SHE WOKE THE NEXT morning. She lifted her chin from Jack's chest as he began to stir and tried to focus on whatever snapped her out of a happy dreamland. A quick glance at the sky told her it was barely dawn. So, what woke her?

"What's going on?" Jack murmured, cupping the back of Ivy's head and pressing a kiss to her forehead. "Are you waking me for sex or a bathroom break? Just for the record, I would prefer sex."

"I don't know," Ivy mumbled, rolling to her side and struggling to a sitting position. "Something woke me up. The last thing I remember was being in a boat with you. We were on a lake in our dream – that was pretty, by the way – and then something ripped me out of our happy place."

"I think your genius is getting away from you," Jack mumbled.

"You woke up, too," Ivy pointed out.

"I woke up because you woke up."

"No, that's not why," Ivy said, grabbing a pair of shorts and a T-shirt from the floor of the tent and shimmying into them. "I think something is going on outside."

"You go and check and I'll wait here," Jack murmured, his eyes closed.

"So much for keeping me safe," Ivy complained, although she left him to his slumber and moved toward the tent flap. They'd attached a bell to it – one of the free bear bells that came with their tent purchase – to alert them if someone tried to get into the tent in the middle of the night. Ivy didn't bother muffling the jangling sound as she left the tent.

When she focused her attention on the campground, she found Scott, Maria, and Donnie standing around the burned out campfire. They were in deep conversation when Ivy approached and they didn't immediately note her arrival.

"I think you're overreacting," Maria said. "We don't know that."

"What's going on?" Ivy asked, stifling a yawn. "Is something wrong?"

Scott licked his lips and glanced at Maria and Donnie before shrugging. "I don't know if something is wrong, but when I woke up this morning, I found Melissa gone," he said. "She's not out here, and we checked the bathroom for her. It's empty."

Ivy knit her eyebrows together as she absorbed the statement. "Are we sure she didn't take a morning walk?"

"Melissa isn't big on walking," Scott said. "You've seen her. The only thing she's wanted to do since she got here is sit by the campfire and drink."

"Do you think we should call someone?" Maria asked.

"What's going on?" Jack asked, tugging on his shirt as he moved in behind Ivy. He looked annoyed at being dragged out of his warm sleeping bag at such an early hour.

"Melissa is missing."

Eighteen

"Run me through this," Jack said, his eyes keen as his gaze bounced from face to face. "What exactly is going on?"

"Run you through what?" Scott challenged. "I went to sleep last night and Melissa was in the camper. I woke up and she was gone."

"That doesn't mean she's missing," Jack protested. "She could be out taking a walk ... or in the bathroom ... or picking up ice at the ranger station. Why did you jump to the conclusion that she's missing?"

"Because it's not even seven in the morning yet and she never gets up before nine," Scott snapped. "She's not a morning person."

"Show me the camper," Jack instructed, following his friend into the large trailer and glancing around. The far end of the camper was elevated, a double bed with messy blankets resting on it. What was supposed to be the table in the kitchen area had been transformed into another bed. The ramifications weren't lost on Jack. "You guys have been sleeping separately."

Scott ran a hand through his morning-tousled hair. "I ... yeah. I slept up in the bed because I have longer legs and she slept down here."

"How much trouble is your marriage in?"

"What does that have to do with anything?" Scott was incensed. "Are you accusing me of doing something to my wife?"

"I'm trying to get a full picture of what's going on here," Jack countered, his voice even and calm. "If we have to call the police – and if she's really missing, we're doing it sooner rather than later – then they're going to ask you the same questions. I can guarantee they're going to be uglier about it than I am."

"The marriage is over," Scott said, rubbing the back of his neck. "It's … been over. We've tried to keep it afloat, but it's just not going to work. This was supposed to be our last trip together. We wanted to hang out with everyone and then announce our separation on the last day. Melissa figured she wouldn't get a chance to see Maria and Lauren again and she wanted to have fun with them before we depressed everyone."

"Was anyone cheating?"

"I … no … why would you ask that?"

"Because you've hit on my girlfriend this week and Melissa threw herself at me when she was drunk," Jack replied. "If the troopers ask when they get here, I'm telling them the truth. You need to tell me the truth."

"I've been sleeping with my secretary," Scott gritted out.

"For how long?"

"Six months."

Ivy silently watched the exchange from the doorway. None of this information surprised her.

"Was Melissa seeing anyone?" Jack asked.

"If you ask her, Melissa claims she didn't know I was sleeping with my secretary until about a month ago," Scott said. "I personally think she was deluding herself, but … whatever. She was extremely angry and said I betrayed her.

"The thing is, I didn't even start looking at my secretary until I was positive Melissa was slipping out on me," he continued. "I wasn't exactly happy up until that point, but I wasn't breaking my vows. She was."

Jack refused to be swayed by Scott's apparent misery. "Who was she seeing?"

"I have no idea."

"I don't believe you," Jack said. "You must have looked at her email ... or cell phone ... or something to see if she was really cheating."

"I did all of that and found nothing."

"So why do you think she was cheating?" Jack pressed.

"Because ... I don't know! It's just a feeling," Scott said. "I can't explain it. I was certain she was cheating, though."

Jack momentarily glanced at Ivy and then shifted his attention back to his friend. "How much did you stand to lose in the divorce?"

"Half of everything."

"What would that have done to you financially?"

"What? Do you think I killed Melissa for money?" Scott was getting angrier by the second.

"Did you?"

"You know what? I can't believe you, Jack," Scott huffed. "We've been friends for ten years. How can you possibly ask me that question?"

"It's my job."

"Really? I can't help but wonder if you're asking because your girl-friend lied to you and said I hit on her," Scott shot back. "I didn't hit on her, by the way. She's not my type. I try to stay away from women who look like strippers."

"You shut your mouth," Jack hissed, taking a menacing step in Scott's direction. "I know you hit on Ivy. In fact, I think you did it twice. She didn't say anything, but she was uncomfortable with what-ever you said to her the day we went kayaking.

"I've seen the way you look at her," he continued. "I'm not blind. Don't lie to me. Don't you dare insult her either. I am this close to walking away from this entire situation and leaving you to deal with it on your own."

Astonished hurt washed over Scott's features. "How is it that you can believe the woman you've been sleeping with for a month over the guy you've been friends with for ten years?"

"Because she doesn't lie to me," Jack replied, unruffled. "I've seen her heart. I've felt it beat while she's sleeping. She's the most loyal and honest person I've ever met. You, on the other hand, can't claim that.

"You were always a fun guy, but you were also a liar," he continued. "You exaggerated about the women you dated, the grades you got, and the future you were going to have. The only thing Ivy exaggerates about is her genius ... and I'm not really sure if that's an exaggeration. I don't want to feed her ego, though, so I want to believe it's an exaggeration. If she's really as smart as she says she is, we're all in trouble."

"You're in trouble when we're alone again," Ivy muttered, crossing her arms over her chest.

"When was the last time you saw Melissa?"

"Last night," Scott said, shooting a hateful look in Ivy's direction. "I hope you're happy. You ruined a friendship."

"Don't you even look at her," Jack warned, wagging a finger in Scott's face. "What time did you go to bed?"

"About an hour after you and Ivy turned in," Scott said.

"Did you go to sleep right away?"

"I did. Melissa read a book. I'm not sure what time she went to bed."

"Did you hear her get up during the night?" Jack asked.

"No," Scott answered, shaking his head. "The camper is small and you can feel when someone moves at either end of it. I slept hard, though. I didn't hear her. If someone dragged her out of here, though, I would've definitely heard that. She had to leave on her own accord."

Jack ran his tongue over his teeth as he considered Scott's statement. "We need to find her," he said. "I'm worried this could go very badly for you if we don't."

"I'm not sure how much worse things can get, Jack," Scott said. "You've picked a woman over your friends and you believe I could've hurt Melissa even though you've known me for ten years. How do things get worse than that?"

"Things can always get worse," Jack said. "Never doubt that."

"THERE'S ABSOLUTELY NOTHING IN THERE," IVY ANNOUNCED,

joining Jack outside the women's bathroom facilities ten minutes later. "I got down on my hands and knees just to make sure. There are no signs of a struggle or blood."

"That's both a good and bad sign," Jack said, eyeing Ivy's hand when she extended it in his direction. "Did you wash your hands after crawling around on the public bathroom floor?"

Ivy scowled. "Fine. Don't hold my hand. I'm sure there are hundreds of people here would like to hold my hand."

"Not if you didn't wash it."

Ivy narrowed her eyes. "Where do you want to head next?"

"I don't know," Jack said, restlessly tugging on the ends of his hair as he glanced around. "I'm starting to think we should call the state police and begin a search right now. We're wasting time."

"Then do that."

"Melissa is a grown woman," Jack pointed out. "She's allowed to voluntarily disappear if she wants to do it. She and Scott obviously had problems – even more than we initially suspected – and maybe it got to be too much for her."

"That's a possibility," Ivy conceded. "Melissa was mortified by what she did. Did you see her last night? She wouldn't make eye contact with you, and the few times she did with me she looked as if she wanted to find a hole to hide in."

"She was definitely embarrassed," Jack said, reaching out and grabbing Ivy's hand. "I'm glad you didn't go after her. That showed tremendous restraint on your part and I appreciate it."

Ivy lifted an eyebrow as she stared at their clasped hands. "I thought you didn't want to get my germs."

Jack forced a watery smile. "I need to touch you," he said. "I'm willing to take my chances."

"What do you think about Scott's story?" Ivy asked. "Do you really think he decided to cheat because he thought Melissa was doing it first?"

"I'm not ruling Melissa cheating out, but I think he's the one who started that game," Jack answered. "I think he was trying to save face for us. He forgets, I watched him cheat on every girlfriend he had in college. He doesn't have a moral compass when it comes to sex."

"Have you ever cheated on a girlfriend?"

Jack shifted so he could study Ivy's face. "No. I'm a firm believer that breaking up with someone – even if it's uncomfortable – is better than betraying them."

"Not even in college?"

"No," Jack said. "What about you?"

"I didn't go to college."

"That's not what I meant, wiseass," Jack teased, tickling Ivy's ribs. "Did you ever cheat on a boyfriend?"

"Before you, I only really ever had one boyfriend," Ivy said. "I never cheated on him, even though he cheated on me. I guess I'm like you. I prefer to remain loyal. If you don't want to be with someone, break up with them. Don't … slip around behind their back."

"I don't think that's ever something you have to worry about with me, honey," Jack said, pulling Ivy in for a quick hug. "I can barely handle you. I don't know what I would do with another mountain of trouble."

"Ha, ha."

Jack kissed her forehead. "You're all I want."

"Me, too."

Jack pressed another quick kiss to Ivy's forehead and then released her. "I'm going to call the state police and alert them to what's going on," he said. "After that, I think we need to start searching the campground."

"Actually, I think you should task the rest of your friends with doing that," Ivy countered. "You and I have to take a hike into the woods."

Jack was surprised. "We do?"

"We have to check the clearing, Jack," Ivy said, swallowing hard. "If someone … took her … there's a good chance she ended up there."

Jack rubbed his thumb over Ivy's cheek, tilting his head to the side as he considered her words. "I don't know why I didn't think of that," he said.

"You've had other things on your mind," Ivy said. "Call Harvey. We'll take this one step at a time."

"I'M GLAD you're with me," Jack said, following Ivy as she moved through the woods.

"Is that because you can't live without my company, or you're afraid of getting lost in the woods?"

"Both," Jack said, squeezing Ivy's hand. "Did you see Scott when we stopped back at the campsite and told them not to wander too far away because we called the state police? He hates me."

"He's in a tough situation, Jack," Ivy said, grabbing his arm and directing him to move around a tree instead of over it.

"Why did you do that?"

"Because that's a mud pit under there," Ivy answered, grabbing a stick and lifting up the fallen leaves to display the sludgy area. "You would've lost your shoe. Even if you got it back, you wouldn't have wanted to wear it."

"If there's ever a zombie apocalypse, I definitely need you on my team," Jack said. "If I'm alone, I might as well step in the mud hole and wait for the zombies to eat me."

"I'll protect you," Ivy said, moving back to the path she was tracing in her head. "As for Scott, he knows he's going to be a suspect if Melissa is dead. If he's innocent, he's still going to feel guilty ... and persecuted ... because he's always going to wonder if he could've saved her. If he's guilty ... well ... he's going to be worrying about saving his ass from here on out. We have to watch him."

"Do you think Melissa is dead?" Jack asked.

"Truthfully?"

"Yes."

"I think she's dead," Ivy confirmed. "I don't know if I can say that I think Scott killed her, though."

"If Scott didn't kill her, that means Donnie or Alex is guilty."

"Not necessarily," Ivy said, pushing her way through a group of trees and striding into the clearing. "I haven't ruled out the women yet."

Jack stilled. "Why would Maria or Lauren kill teenage girls?"

"You're looking at it as if there's a sexual component," Ivy pointed out. "We're not sure there is yet."

"I guess that's true," Jack said, rubbing his stubbled chin. "If what you're saying is true, then we've been going about this all wrong. We need to draw the women in and feel them out, too."

"I have been doing that," Ivy said. "We can't focus on that now, though. There's no body here. That doesn't mean there's not a clue here. Let's split up and look around."

"I don't think we should split up."

"It's a small clearing, Jack. You'll hear me if I need you."

"No," Jack said, shaking his head. "We're in this together, Ivy. Let's look around … together." Jack held out his hand and watched as Ivy reluctantly took it.

"You know I didn't wash my hands, right?"

"You make me tired sometimes," Jack muttered.

Nineteen

"Is this all you found?" Trooper Harvey asked an hour later, gesturing toward the scattering of blood on the far side of the clearing.

Jack nodded. "We looked around the area, but when we found the blood we stopped wandering around," he said. "We didn't want to mess up what could be a potential crime scene."

"That was smart on your part," Harvey said. "You know this makes three dead people you've found, right, Ms. Morgan? If I was a less trusting man, I would throw you in jail right now just to cut down on my workload."

Ivy balked. "We don't know for sure that Melissa is dead," she pointed out. "We don't even know for sure that this is human blood."

"Do you think an animal killed another animal and then cleaned up the carcass mess when he was done munching? If so, I would love to hire him as a maid. I'll bet I can get a real deal on him."

"Don't talk to her like that," Jack intoned, narrowing his eyes. "We're trying to help. In case you've forgotten, Melissa is married to one of my oldest friends."

"A friend that may or may not be a murderer," Harvey clarified. "Did you tell your friends what I told you yesterday?"

"Not exactly," Jack hedged.

"Do you want to expand on that?" Harvey asked. The trio was alone while they waited for the state police's evidence collection unit to arrive. They were running out of ways to pretend they liked one another.

"Ivy suggested mixing up the truth with a few lies when we talked to them last night," Jack explained. "We wanted to gauge their reactions, you know, see if anyone showed an overt interest in the case."

Harvey expectantly crossed his arms over his chest.

"We didn't admit that the bones belonged to a teenage girl," Jack said. "We said you didn't give us that information, but you did believe the two cases were linked. We also said that you were looking at last year's visitor list so you could compare it to this year's list."

"That was smart," Harvey said. "If you told them we already knew they were all here both years someone might've been suspicious of you. Did any of them act differently after you told them that?"

"Ironically, they were all interested in that little tidbit," Jack admitted. "I don't know what to think."

"Scott knew it was a teenage girl," Ivy reminded him. "That jumped out at you."

"That's true," Jack conceded. "He did mention that it was a teenage girl even though we never supplied him with that information."

"What did he say when you called him on it?"

"He claimed that he assumed it was a teenage girl because Ivy volunteered that you guys were investigating the cases as if they were linked," Jack replied. "He assumed one killer would be after the same kind of victim."

"I guess that's plausible," Harvey said. "I think it's a little coincidental that his wife turned up missing later that night."

"You need to question him," Jack said. "They've been having marital problems and he told me this morning that they agreed to divorce and were just waiting to tell everyone at the end of the week."

"Infidelity?"

Jack nodded. "He claims it was on both of their parts, but Melissa isn't around to back that up," he said. "I can say that Melissa threw herself at me the day before yesterday when she was drunk. She said her husband wasn't interested in her and she wanted to ... let off some steam. I turned her down and she passed out early. Scott has also hit on Ivy ... at least once."

"Is that out of the ordinary for him?" Harvey asked. "More specifically, to your knowledge, has he gone after someone else's girlfriend before?"

Jack shrugged. "I mean ... it was hard to keep up with the women he was with when we were in college, but that's college," he said. "I don't specifically remember him going after someone else's girlfriend, and he certainly never went after the women I dated."

"Did you warn him off about going after Ms. Morgan?"

"I did," Jack confirmed. "I told him to stay away from her."

"He doesn't sound like much of a friend."

"I don't know that I would call him a true friend," Jack said. "The thing is ... when you're friends with someone in college, those relationships change as you pick different career paths and move to different parts of the state. We've kept in touch, but it's not like I see any of them regularly."

"And this is the first time you've met any of them?" Harvey asked, shifting his attention to Ivy.

"Yes."

"Have you noticed anything strange about these people?" Harvey pressed. "You're an outsider, so you would have a unique take on how they interact."

"They seem close in some respects, and ... distant ... in others," Ivy answered, opting for honesty. "I think everyone is putting on an act for everyone else. They all want to prove they're happy and successful, but I'm not sure how happy any of them really are."

"You two seem happy," Harvey pointed out. "How are you guys interacting with everyone?"

"Very carefully," Jack said. "My relationship with Ivy was a surprise for them. I used to be a police detective down in Detroit ... and I was injured in the line of duty ... and I was not in a good place when I moved to Shadow Lake. They didn't realize I was dating anyone, and when I showed up with Ivy they were all surprised."

"I'm aware of your history, Detective Harker," Harvey said. "I ran your background after the first body was found. You're a hero, and you have my respect. I am worried that you and Ms. Morgan seem to be in the thick of things, though. Have you considered separating yourself from the situation?"

"If I think it becomes necessary to leave, I will," Jack said. "Keeping Ivy safe is my first priority. If I leave now, though, that's pretty much the equivalent of wiping my hands of them forever. I'm not sure if I'm ready to do that."

"I can't say I blame you," Harvey said. "For now, you need to keep your eyes and ears open. If we get any information, I'll call you with it. There might be a way we can work together to smoke the guilty party out."

"What about Melissa?" Ivy asked.

"All we have is a missing woman and blood right now," Harvey replied. "We won't be certain if it's Melissa's blood – or human, for that matter – for several hours. Right now, everyone needs to remain vigilant. That's all we can do."

"I CAN'T believe I let you talk me into this," Jack grumbled, picking his way through the tall grass and following Ivy toward Andrew Devlin's forest shack. "Don't you think we should go back to the campground and join in the search for Melissa?"

"We're going to do that after we check on Andrew," Ivy replied, tugging on her limited patience and silently reminding herself that Jack was in turmoil and he didn't mean to sound so whiny. "He might have heard something."

"Or he might have *done* something."

"I heard that," Ivy snapped. "You said yourself that you thought he was a good guy. It won't hurt to drop in on him. He knows these woods better than anyone. It won't take long."

"Fine."

"You know what?" Ivy ceased her forward momentum and planted her hands on her hips. She hadn't bothered putting makeup on – not that she often did – and her hair was a mess, but she was still the prettiest woman Jack had ever laid eyes on in real life. "If you don't want to come with me, you don't have to. Why don't you sit here in this field and feel sorry for yourself. I will find you when I'm done."

Jack narrowed his eyes. "That's not going to happen."

"Then stop complaining!"

"You're hot when you get angry," Jack said, catching Ivy off guard. "I think that's why we fight so much."

Despite the surreal nature of the conversation, Ivy found herself blushing. "We fight because we both like it," she countered. "It gets our blood boiling and gives us ideas about ways to make up. It's just the way we're both built."

"Have you noticed that everyone else – and I'm talking couples here – seems to have problems and yet they put on brave faces and pretend they don't?" Jack asked, shifting gears as he fell into step beside Ivy. "You and I fight out our problems in public, and we're happier because we do. They all hide their problems, and they seem miserable. I mean … do you think any of them are happy?"

"That's an interesting question," Ivy replied. "We know Scott and Melissa aren't happy. When I look at Maria and Alex I see two strangers sharing a marriage. They rarely interact."

"Huh. You're right," Jack said, racking his brain for a single instance where he saw Maria and Alex enjoy each other's company over the past few days. "They were together to put up their tent on the day everyone arrived. Since then, Maria has spent almost all of her time with Lauren and Alex has spent almost all of his with Donnie and Scott."

"Maria was also extremely snarky when I met her," Ivy reminded him. "She had plenty to say about Donnie's relationship with Lauren and how it wasn't going to last if he didn't propose, and she also had nasty things to say about Scott and Melissa. She never said a thing about her own husband."

"That's a pretty interesting observation, honey," Jack said. "I can't remember Alex saying anything about her either."

"You never told me how your fishing excursion went," Ivy prodded. "What did you guys talk about?"

"Sports."

Ivy scowled and made a disgusted sound in the back of her throat. "Men."

"We might have talked about you a little bit, too," Jack conceded. "You're very popular with them."

"That's probably because they've all seen me naked."

"Don't remind me of that," Jack said. "I want to be the only one who has ever seen you naked."

"You're pretty close to being the only one."

"Good," Jack said, slinging an arm around her shoulders. "They were curious about the nursery and Max. They asked if I met your parents and whether or not they liked me. They wanted to know how I kept myself busy in Shadow Lake."

"Did you get a creepy vibe off any of them?"

Jack chuckled. "Not really," he answered. "In fact, that fishing extravaganza is the one time I can say things felt like they used to between the four of us. It was a nice throwback to a different time."

"And that's because the women weren't around," Ivy said. "I'm telling you, we can't rule Maria and Lauren out in this. One of them could be crazy. In fact ... have you considered that Melissa faked her own disappearance because she's the guilty party?"

Jack faltered, stunned disbelief washing over him. The more he thought about it, though, the more Ivy's words churned through his head and intrigued him. "I actually hadn't considered that," he said. "How would she do it?"

"Well, we laid the groundwork for whoever is guilty to go off the rails when we told that story around the campfire last night," Ivy supplied, warming to her theory. "We know Melissa has been struggling. What if she waited until she was sure Scott was asleep to slip out? She could have cut herself to leave the trail of blood, and then taken off ... maybe hitched a ride or something once she got out to the highway.

"If she was really bitter about Scott cheating on her, she might think he deserves being framed for the murders," she continued. "This would be a way to fake her own death and start a new life and still get away with murder."

"It's an interesting theory," Jack said. "It's missing a motive, though. Why would Melissa kill two female teenagers?"

"I have no idea," Ivy admitted. "I was just kind of spitballing."

"You're cute when you spitball," Jack said. "No matter what Harvey is keeping

to himself, I have to believe there's a sexual component to this. Otherwise I can't come up with a motive for anyone."

"Maybe Melissa is a closet lesbian."

"She hit on me."

"Don't remind me of that," Ivy instructed. "It still bothers me, and if she is dead, that means I'm having evil thoughts about a murder victim. That makes me feel bad."

"Duly noted," Jack said.

"Besides, maybe she thought you looked like a manly woman and that's what turns her on," Ivy added. "Did you ever think of that?"

Ivy didn't wait to hear his answer, instead scampering out of his reach when he chased her. She didn't stop until she was in Andrew's front yard. The area looked empty, but that didn't stop Ivy from calling out."

"Andrew!" She waited for an answer, but when she didn't hear one she suggested looking around. "What could it hurt?"

"We are not breaking into that man's house," Jack argued. "I'm a police officer. That's against the law."

"I was not suggesting breaking into his house, you big baby," Ivy shot back. "I was suggesting looking around the property. While I don't think Andrew is guilty – and I know you have your doubts about his innocence – I wouldn't put it past one of your friends to try and frame him. Maybe whoever it is killed Melissa and dumped her out here."

"That's another interesting theory," Jack said. "How did they know where to find the shack? I couldn't find my way back here if you wrapped yourself in nothing but bacon, hid on the property, and told me I could have as much of you and the bacon as I wanted if I found you."

"Wow. That is a visual I will never be able to get out of my head. You've traumatized me for life."

"What freaks you out more?" Jack asked. "Is it the bacon or the naked hide and seek?"

"If you want to play naked hide and seek, we can do it by my house when I can be assured that we won't be discovered," Ivy said. "I will never, not under any circumstances, wrap myself in animal meat for you. That's where I draw the line."

"I can live with that," Jack said. "I think naked hide and seek sounds like an absolutely great way to spend a weekend night. We can build a bonfire and strip before playing our game."

"I recommend playing with underwear on," Ivy countered. "You can't see Poison Ivy in the dark."

"Now I know you're a genius, honey."

"Try not forgetting it this time."

Twenty

❧

"He's not here," Ivy said forty minutes later, frustrated. "There's nothing here."

"What was your first clue?" Jack asked. He fought the urge to remind Ivy he didn't want to search for Devlin in the first place. He didn't think an "I was right and you were wrong" argument would be the best way to spend the rest of the day.

"Where do you think he is?" Ivy asked, casting one more look over her shoulder and then letting Jack lead her back in the direction of the campground.

"He could be out walking, or fishing ... or hiding a body."

"You're not funny," Ivy muttered, knitting her eyebrows together as she moved to yank her hand away from Jack. He didn't let her, instead focusing on the obstinate tilt of her chin. Something was really bothering her.

"Can I ask you something?"

"Not if you're going to make fun of me."

"I promise I don't want to make fun of you," Jack said. "Why are you so ... invested ... in Andrew Devlin?"

"I'm not!"

"You are, honey," Jack argued. "You're worried about him. You're interested in what he's doing. I love your heart, and you go out of your way to help people whenever you can, but for some reason you're digging your heels in on Andrew Devlin. I want to know why."

"I ... ." Ivy broke off. She didn't know how to answer him. She wanted to argue with his assertion, but she realized he had a point. "I guess I see some of myself in him." It was hard to admit, but there it was.

"How so?"

"People judge him by how he looks," Ivy answered. "I judged him by how he looks when I first saw him. I was afraid."

"Okay," Jack said, unsure what she was getting at.

"Hayden thought he was a werewolf," Ivy said. "He didn't seem surprised by that. He's used to people looking at him and seeing something he's not. People make knee jerk reactions because he looks different. I guess I ... relate to that."

"Honey, I admit that I've been ... judgmental ... where Andrew is concerned," Jack said. "It's not because of the way he looks, though. I don't like my girlfriend wandering off with any stranger.

"As for the other stuff, when I first moved to Shadow Lake, Brian told me that you have always been different," he continued. "That's not a bad thing. That's a wonderful thing, especially when it comes to you."

"That's nice of you to say, but you heard Scott this morning," Ivy said. "He said I look like a stripper."

"You don't look like a stripper."

"Somehow I think I should be insulted by that," Ivy said. "I don't look normal. You can't say I do. I have pink streaks in my hair and I like to wear ankle-length skirts without shoes. I ... set myself apart on purpose."

"I think you do that because you're different and that's your way of acknowledging it," Jack said. "Your heart is different. That's why it's so wonderful. You make yourself look different because you want people to stay away from you. It's a warning.

"You know, we've learned some interesting things about you since we met," he continued. "You can dream walk."

"So can you!"

"You said I was calling you into my dreams," Jack clarified. "You provided the magic for us to join up in our subconscious thoughts. I know that. I can play the dream game with you if I really concentrate, but you're still making it happen.

"When you add that to the fact that you managed to talk to Laura's ghost when she was displaced from her body by her brother, the only conclusion we can come to is that you're magic," he continued. "I knew you were magic the first time I saw you. You're also the prettiest woman I've ever seen. You're not strange. You're wonderful."

"Maybe Andrew is wonderful, too," Ivy suggested.

"He would have to be to elicit such a loyal reaction from you," Jack said. "I'm sorry I didn't take your feelings into consideration. I honestly don't believe Andrew is involved. He's not stupid enough to kill someone in his own back yard and then direct you toward the body."

"Okay."

"Listen, my magical wonder, I like that you're different," Jack said. "I'm different, too. You can see that and you like me all the same. Try to have faith that someone can feel the same way about you. Perhaps we're two oddballs who found each other at the exact right moment in time. That makes both of us magic."

"You're a romantic at heart, Jack."

"Only with you, honey."

"THANK GOD you're back," Maria announced, swiveling with her hands on her hips and fixing Jack and Ivy with a dark look as they approached. "What were you thinking taking off like that when Melissa is missing?"

"We were thinking that we had to check the clearing where the first body was found and talk to the state police," Jack replied, not missing a beat. "What's going on here?"

"Oh." Maria straightened. "I ... we're in crisis mode here."

"I'll bet," Jack said. "Have the state troopers been by?"

"They questioned us for two hours," Lauren complained, rolling her eyes as she sat in a chair close to the campfire. "It was almost as if they suspected us of doing something to Melissa ... like we would ever do that."

"They're doing their jobs," Jack said. "Where is Scott?"

"Oh, he's over there," Maria said, pointing toward a pine tree on the far side of the campsite. "He's been drinking for an hour straight."

"That seems like a great why to look for his missing wife," Jack said.

"Hey, we've been all over this campground asking questions about Melissa," Donnie argued. "Alex is still out questioning people. No one saw her. Well, I guess we don't know that for a fact. If someone did see her, though, they're not telling us."

"What did you find?" Maria asked. "Do the police have any leads?"

"We found fresh blood in the clearing, but no body," Jack replied, opting not to mince words. "The volume wasn't enough to say definitively that whoever lost it is dead. The state police are running it through their crime lab. There's still a chance that the blood isn't human."

"I have no idea what any of that means," Maria said. "Why don't you try and dumb it down for the little people."

"Don't be a pain," Jack chided. "We don't know a lot. We know Melissa went into the camper before eleven. We know that between eleven and six she disappeared. We don't know if she walked out of the camper on her own or whether she was dragged out.

"We know that we found fresh blood in the clearing," he continued. "It wasn't enough to declare anyone dead. We don't know if belongs to an actual human. We know that Scott and Melissa were going to get divorced and he has a motive. That's basically where we're at."

Maria's mouth dropped open, and Jack realized his mistake when it was too late to yank the words back into his mouth.

"Scott and Melissa are getting divorced? Holy crap! Why didn't anyone tell us?" Maria was practically screeching.

"I thought you said the state troopers stopped by," Jack prodded. "Didn't they question Scott about the impending divorce when they were here?"

"They separated us for questioning," Lauren supplied, suddenly interested in the conversation. "I can't believe they're really getting divorced. Do you know why?"

Jack cast a glance in Scott's direction. The man seemed lost in his own little world, his only friend consisting of the can of beer he clutched in his hand. "I should probably let Scott tell you this, but he seems ... lost ... right now," Jack said. "He said that he suspected Melissa of cheating on him so he started sleeping with his secretary. He claims they were unhappy before that, though. They recently agreed to the divorce and were going to tell everyone at the end of the week."

"Why didn't they mention anything?" Lauren asked.

Ivy couldn't help but notice how much happier Lauren seemed now that she had something to gossip about.

"I don't know," Jack replied. "You'll have to ask Scott ... when he sobers up. Did Melissa mention anything to you guys about cheating on Scott?"

"No," Maria said, immediately shaking her head.

"We did have suspicions, though," Lauren said. "She's been acting odd for months."

"Define odd."

"Melissa has always been the quiet sort," Maria supplied. "She doesn't volunteer information. Everything we know about her ... well ... we've had to kind of figure it out on our own."

"How does that work if you don't have information?" Ivy asked.

"When you're a woman, it's easy to figure that stuff out," Lauren said, causing Ivy to bite the inside of her cheek to hold in a scathing retort. "Melissa has been unhappy for a long time, but we thought the marriage would last because she got status through Scott's job."

"He's a stockbroker," Jack said. "What kind of status is attached to that?"

"It wasn't about the job," Maria clarified. "It was the money. He brought a lot of money into the household and he was convinced he was going to be named a partner in his firm. He was up for a promotion about a year ago, and he thought for sure he was going to get it.

"Melissa had big plans for when he got that promotion," she continued. "She had a house in a gated community all picked out. It had a saltwater pool and a sauna in the basement. She wouldn't stop talking about it."

"She was lording it over us, you mean," Maria corrected. "Since Scott made more money than Alex and Donnie, she always acted as if she was doing us a favor hanging out with us. Well, when the date for the promotion came and went, we asked her what happened."

"She didn't want to tell us," Lauren said, clearly enjoying the gossip session. "Finally, after about three bottles of wine, she admitted that Scott didn't get the promotion. She had a lot of excuses, but apparently it came down to his attitude. The boss doesn't like him."

"I think she realized that Scott was never going to make the money she'd been dreaming about after that," Maria said. "She became … withdrawn. We didn't see each other a lot, but the guys try to meet up once a month and we get dragged along for every trip. Every time we saw her after that she was more and more morose."

"But she never mentioned seeing someone else?" Jack pressed.

"Never."

"What about Scott? Did you know he was seeing someone else?"

"No," Lauren replied. "It doesn't surprise me, though. He's always been a player. I'm not sure he's the type who can ever be faithful."

Jack shifted his eyes to Ivy. "What do you think?"

"I think it's like a soap opera," Ivy replied. "Every time we think we have everything figured out, some diva comes wandering around to shake things up."

"I'M EXHAUSTED, HONEY," JACK SAID, RUBBING IVY'S BACK AS they cuddled next to the fire shortly before ten. "Do you mind calling it a night?"

"That sounds like a good idea," Ivy said, stifling a yawn. "Everyone else has already separated and turned in for the night. Scott passed out four hours ago."

"I don't think that call I got from Harvey made things better," Jack said.

"We know the blood in the clearing belongs to Melissa," Ivy said. "That doesn't mean she's dead."

"You're the one who told me earlier that you thought she was dead. Did you forget that?"

"I still believe she's dead," Ivy clarified. "For your sake – and the sake of your friends – I hope that she's not. Maybe something will happen that can explain all of this."

"Or maybe she's dead and someone just did a better job of hiding her body this time," Jack suggested.

"Why?"

"What do you mean why? The state police showed up after the last body was found and then we discovered the first body," Jack said. "Someone obviously wants to ease the police presence."

"Then why kidnap a woman so close to the other incident?"

"I … huh. I honestly have no idea."

"There's a lot here we don't understand, Jack," Ivy said. "We're not going to figure it out tonight. Let's get some sleep and look at it fresh in the morning. We're both too tired to see the big picture."

"That sounds like the best suggestion I've heard all day," Jack said. "I have to go to the bathroom first. How about you?"

"Yes, please, sir."

Jack grinned. "How about I allow you to go on your side of the building all by yourself while I go on my side? I promise not to wait outside for you and act like a nervous boyfriend."

"I guess that will have to do," Ivy said, pushing herself to a standing position. "I need sleep, and you're never going to let me walk over there alone."

"You've got that right."

IVY FIGURED JACK WOULD BE WAITING FOR HER OUTSIDE OF THE bathroom when she exited, but instead she found silence. She started moving toward the other side of the building – the men's facilities were on the opposite side of the square structure – but something stopped her in her tracks.

Ivy swiveled quickly, her skin prickling. Someone was watching her. She could feel it. She opened her mouth to call out but snapped it shut when Jack appeared in front of her.

"Are you ready for bed, honey?"

Ivy considered telling him what she felt, and then discarded the notion. Even if someone was watching her, that didn't mean it was a killer. It was probably another camper. They were both tired. Sleep was more important that forcing Jack to skulk around the bushes looking for something that probably wasn't there.

"I'm definitely ready," Ivy replied. "I think we should just sleep tonight. No dream interludes. I need to shut my brain off."

"That's fine with me," Jack said. "I have you in real life. I already have the dream."

Twenty-One

"We both have to shower before we do anything else today," Ivy announced the next morning, ruefully tugging on her hair and making a face as she studied it. "We smell."

"And good morning to you, too, honey," Jack deadpanned, rolling his neck until it cracked. "I'll have you know, I don't smell. I'm manly and that thing you think you're smelling is manliness."

"We haven't showered in two days," Ivy countered. "We have to shower. That's what we're doing before anything else."

"What about breakfast?"

"I'm not cooking for you until you don't stink."

"You're a mean woman, honey," Jack said, although he lifted his arm and sniffed to make sure she wasn't exaggerating. "You're kind of right, though. Okay, I guess you'll be safe showering when it's light out. You have to promise to do your business over there and then immediately come over here and wait for me in the tent."

"Or I could start breakfast so we can eat," Ivy countered. "Your stomach was growling for half the night."

"I think it was just talking so you wouldn't be lonely."

"You're in a good mood given what we're going to be going through today," Ivy said. "How come?"

"You make me happy," Jack replied, tugging her face close so he could kiss her. "After looking at my friends and the lies they've been living, I can't tell you how happy I am to have you."

"Okay, you're definitely getting bacon this morning," Ivy said. "I can't promise to wrap myself in it, but I do promise to cook it."

"Thank you!" Jack kissed her again. "Gather your stuff, stinky. Make sure you have absolutely everything you need. You're not allowed to wander back and forth once I'm in the shower. Promise me."

"I promise," Ivy said. "Right now, a long shower to wash off the filth sounds absolutely heavenly."

"The only thing that would make it better is if we could do it together," Jack said. "Come on. Let's start our day."

By the time Ivy and Jack climbed out of their tent, everyone else was gathered around the freshly revitalized fire. They all looked as if deep conversation was on the menu, and no one was happy about it.

"What's going on?" Jack asked, shuffling his shower essentials to one arm and ushering Ivy forward with the other. "Did something happen? Did the state troopers come by?"

"No," Donnie replied, handing Scott a bottle of water. The man looked like death warmed over, and whatever hangover he was battling appeared to be getting the better of him. "We were all discussing leaving."

Jack stilled. "Excuse me?"

"We can't stay here," Lauren said. "Melissa is missing and probably dead. A teenage girl was mutilated and ripped apart. This has officially been the worst vacation ever."

"Let me get this straight, you've decided to deal with Melissa's disappearance by running away?" Jack was beyond irked. "What are you even thinking?"

"We're thinking that this place isn't safe," Maria said. "Any one of us could be next."

"Scott, are you considering leaving knowing that your wife is missing and might be out there?" Ivy asked, genuinely curious.

Scott shifted his red-rimmed eyes to Ivy. "What do you care? You've broken this friendship. I don't have to tell you anything."

"Don't speak to her like that," Jack snapped. "I'm warning you. If you do it again, I'm going to punch you. I don't care how hungover you are."

"You can't talk to me like that," Scott shot back. "I'm not one of your criminals, Jack. I have rights."

"You do," Jack confirmed. "Apparently you're exercising your right to abandon your missing wife and go back to your life. You know what? More power to you. You make me sick."

"What do you want me to do, Jack?" Scott spat. "She's gone. We all know she's dead. How long are we supposed to sit here and wait for someone else to die?"

"Why do you think anyone here is a target?" Ivy challenged.

"Obviously we're targets," Lauren said. "That's why Melissa was taken from our camp."

"We don't know that," Jack argued. "She might have gotten up to go to the bathroom in the middle of the night and gotten taken over there. She might have wandered off on her own and got taken at the other end of the campground. We don't know anything."

"Dude, I can't lie," Donnie said. "I'm terrified. I'm not just terrified for myself, but I don't feel like Lauren is safe here."

"I feel the same way about Maria," Alex said. "I'm actually surprised that you're so gung-ho to stay here, Jack. Aren't you worried about Ivy's safety? She has found two bodies, after all. She might make a very appealing target."

"I'm always worried about Ivy's safety," Jack replied. "That's why I'm keeping her close. If you guys want to leave, I can't stop you. I can seriously question what type of people you are, though, but I've been doing that for days.

"The truth is, the state troopers are looking at all of us," he continued. "Anyone leaving under these circumstances when their wife and close friend is missing is going to draw more attention to themselves. Go nuts. Leave. I don't really care at this point."

"Are you going to stay?" Maria asked.

"We're staying until we find out what happened to Melissa," Jack answered. "My conscious won't let me do anything else."

"I HAVE AN IDEA," IVY ANNOUNCED WHEN JACK JOINED HER AT the picnic table forty minutes later.

"I think a nap sounds great," Jack said. "I missed you in my dreams last night, although the nine hours of sleep did us both good. You have color back in your cheeks. I was a little worried that you were wearing yourself down after so much excitement. You were really pale."

"That's because I convinced myself someone was watching me before you showed up outside of the bathroom."

Jack pursed his lips. "You really know how to ruin a moment, don't you?"

"I decided I was imagining it," Ivy said. "I didn't want you wandering around in the dark when I was merely working myself into a lather because I was tired."

"Ivy, I refuse to fight with you today, so I'm not going to yell," Jack said, watching as she placed bacon in the skillet. "You're also cooking me bacon, and I don't want to risk you taking it away. You have to promise me that you're going to tell me the next time you think someone is watching you."

"Even if I'm sure I'm imagining it?"

"Yes," Jack answered. "I would rather be safe than sorry."

"Okay," Ivy said, holding her hands up in a placating manner. "I promise I will tell you whenever I think someone is watching me."

"Thank you."

"Maria is watching me right now," Ivy said, inclining her chin toward Maria and Alex's tent. "Beat her up."

"You're so cute," Jack said, tweaking Ivy's nose. "At least they've agreed to stay. They're not happy about it, but I think my admission that they'd be considered suspects if they left forced them all to make a tough decision."

"They're covering their tracks," Ivy said. "It's all about appearances with them."

"I'm starting to get that," Jack said. "Wait ... didn't you just say you had an idea?"

"I *do* have an idea," Ivy said, handing the skillet to Jack. "I think we should take kayaks out and scan the shoreline."

"Why?"

"Because that would be a really easy way to discard a body," Ivy answered. "Think about it. The kayaks are located two sites down. You're supposed to sign them out at the ranger station, but someone could easily take one in the middle of the night and put it back without anyone being the wiser."

"That's an interesting idea, honey," Jack said. "We both know that all three of our suspects know how to use a kayak. My problem is that the openings are so narrow that I think it would be practically impossible to get a body and a man inside of one."

"Not if they draped the body over the kayak and secured it with a rope."

"Okay, let's say I'm entertaining this for a moment," Jack said. "You're basically suggesting that someone killed Melissa here and then dragged her to a kayak, tied her to it, and then paddled out across the lake to dispose of her body."

"That's exactly what I'm suggesting."

"Then how did Melissa's blood end up in the clearing?"

"Maybe someone collected it from her body before dumping her and placed it in the clearing to serve as a distraction," Ivy suggested. "Someone is working overtime to confuse law enforcement. Even though she was a thin woman, Melissa's dead weight would've been impossible for one person to carry that far into the woods without help.

"No matter how annoying I find most of the people here right now — especially given their cowardly natures — I don't see more than one of them being guilty," she continued. "They're too gossipy. They never would've been able to keep it secret."

"So you think Melissa's body is somewhere close to the lake, but on the other side," Jack surmised.

"Exactly."

"Well, honey, I've learned never to ignore your intuition," Jack said. "Let's eat breakfast and pack a picnic lunch. That will give us an excuse to stay out all afternoon. Let's see if you really are a genius."

"**I DON'T** KNOW HOW WE'RE SUPPOSED TO NARROW THIS down," Jack said two hours later. He lazily floated next to Ivy as she studied the nearby shoreline. His second try in a kayak was going much smoother than the first. It still bothered him that Ivy was so much better at controlling her small craft than he was.

"I think we can rule out the east and west sides of the lake," Ivy said, her face screwed up in concentration. "They're both filled with houses. Someone would have to be stupid to dump a body there."

"That leaves the south side of the lake," Jack said. "Do you see anything over there that piques your interest?"

"I do," Ivy confirmed.

Jack was surprised. "Really? What?"

Ivy pointed at the dock. "That's a summer camp," she said. "I know because I went there when I was a kid. It's abandoned. The state is trying to sell the land to a developer. He wants to put condos there and the neighbors around the lake are fighting it."

"How do you know that?"

"It's been all over the television," Ivy replied. "At night, there's a light on that dock. It's not bright, but it does serve as a landmark. If someone was crossing the lake at night, they would need something to focus on so they didn't get lost or turned around. What better than a lighted dock?"

"Okay, you've convinced me," Jack said. "Take me to the dock."

It took the couple about fifteen minutes to navigate across the lake, and Ivy made sure to secure both kayaks at the end of the dock before joining Jack on the shore. He glanced around the deserted camp, seemingly entranced, and jolted when Ivy appeared beside him.

"I didn't mean to frighten you," Ivy said. "I thought you heard me coming."

"I was just thinking," Jack said. "I'll bet this was a cool place to visit when you were a kid. In the city, we don't have anything like this. Any camps they have down there are held at community centers and metroparks. This place is really amazing."

"I didn't really like summer camp because I had to sleep in a cabin with a bunch of girls I didn't like," Ivy said. "I was fine when I could mingle out in the open, but I felt like I was being smothered at night."

"Well, I think we should rent a cabin on a lake one weekend and do our own version of summer camp so we can both enjoy it," Jack suggested. "It doesn't have to be this lake ... and I'm going to be honest, if we never come back here, I'll be a happy man. I still think it would be fun to do."

"I think that's a great idea," Ivy said. "I would love that."

"Good," Jack said, dropping a soft kiss on her lips. "The problem with this camp is that it's big. There are a lot of places to hide a body."

"It can't be too far away," Ivy said, glancing around. "It has to be in a spot where it can be hidden from prying eyes and yet still easily accessible from the dock. After all the energy expended killing a woman and paddling her body across the lake, the killer would have to be exhausted."

"Okay, so where?"

Ivy pointed toward an old maintenance shed. The building was ramshackle and the roof looked as if it was about to cave in. "You could put a body in there easily and potential developers would never bother looking inside because they would tear it down."

Jack moved in that direction, his face grim as he closed the distance. He studied the door handle for a moment, and then lifted his shirt to cover his hand. "Just in case there's a chance of getting finger-prints," he said.

Ivy watched, her heart constricting as he pulled open the door. She smelled the evidence of her purported genius before she saw it. Jack stuck his head inside briefly and then shut the door.

"It's Melissa," Jack said, pressing his eyes shut briefly. "I have to call Harvey."

"He's going to be really annoyed."

"Not half as annoyed as I am," Jack said. "Someone stabbed her through the throat. That's where they got the blood."

"We have a body," Ivy said, pinching her nose to ward off the lingering stench. "Now we just have to find the murderer."

"And I have to look at my own friends to do it," Jack said.

Twenty-Two

"**I** hear you two have been busy."

Brian Nixon stared at Jack and Ivy through the computer screen, his face hard to read thanks to his distance from the tiny camera, but his grin was unmistakable. They were linked via Skype to make the discussion easier, but now Jack wished he'd placed a regular phone call so he wouldn't have to put up with his partner's smug smile.

"We've had better weeks," Jack conceded, weariness overtaking him. "What have you got for us?"

Jack and Ivy sat in an isolated office at the state trooper command center in Gaylord, Trooper Harvey coming close to blowing a gasket when they called him with the location of Melissa's body. When he arrived on scene he was beside himself, cursing a blue streak as he called Jack and Ivy every name in the book.

He was off dealing with his boss right now, and Jack expected another tongue lashing before the day was out. He couldn't worry about that now, though.

"I'll bet you wish you wouldn't have taken my advice to ask Ivy camping since all of this has happened," Brian said.

Jack scowled while Ivy lifted her eyebrows.

"Your advice? I thought you wanted me to go camping with you?" Ivy's expression was bouncing between angry and sad.

"I *did* want you to go camping with me," Jack said. "I was just afraid to ask you. Brian convinced me I was being an idiot." Jack turned his furious countenance on an amused Brian. "Don't put ideas in her head. I have enough going on without you making things worse."

"He's telling the truth, Ivy," Brian said. "He was a nervous wreck about asking you. It was kind of cute. He was considering canceling the entire trip because he couldn't bear the thought of being away from you."

"Sadly, I think we would've had more fun at home," Ivy said. "I did take him to Call of the Wild, though."

"No kidding?" Brian's eyes lit up. "You loved that place as a kid. I remember taking all of you one weekend when it was raining and we had nothing better to do and you spent hours wandering through that gift shop. I think you could've lived there."

"Jack thought it was fun."

"I did think it was fun," Jack agreed, brushing Ivy's hair away from her face. "We're going back when things aren't so ... messed up. Speaking of that, please tell me you have information."

"I have a lot of information," Brian said. "I'm not sure what's important, though. There's a lot of stuff here."

"Start with Scott," Jack prodded. "His wife is dead so he's the primary suspect."

"Okay, Scott Graham lives in a suburb of Detroit called Pleasant Ridge," Brian said. "It looks fairly affluent, but his monetary situation suggests he may be living over his means."

"We heard gossip about that yesterday," Jack said. "Apparently Scott was up for a promotion at his firm and Melissa had her heart set on some huge house in a gated community, but it all fell through because Scott didn't get the promotion."

"I think your friend Melissa had a shopping problem," Brian said. "I see a lot of activity on their credit cards. My understanding is that she worked as a paralegal for a law firm. She made okay money, but not enough to support her shoe habit. Scott is teetering on the edge of bankruptcy. His entire house of cards could topple at any time."

"Was there a life insurance policy on Melissa?" Ivy asked.

"Good question, honey," Jack said, tugging her down on his lap so they could get comfortable for the rest of the conversation.

"You two are just as sickly sweet from afar," Brian complained, making a face. "There is a life insurance policy. It's worth a half a million bucks."

"Is that enough to dig Scott out of his financial problems?"

"Just barely," Brian answered. "He would be able to pay off his debt, but he wouldn't have much left to play around with."

"That could be motive," Jack suggested. "Scott has always cared about appearances. If Melissa divorced him and got half of everything, they would both lose the status they coveted."

"Melissa seemed more interested in that status than Scott," Ivy pointed out. "I'm surprised they didn't come up with some agreement to stay in the marriage for appearances and live separate lives at the same time."

"Maybe this boyfriend Scott is convinced she was floating the idea of marrying him," Jack said. "He might've had more money so Melissa wasn't afraid to walk away from Scott."

"Well, I've been through Melissa's phone records and I can't find a boyfriend in there," Brian said. "She talks to some friends in a book club quite often, but they're all female and I think the book club is code for drinking and complaining about people. That's all they seem to do in their text messages. She's also on the phone with Maria fairly regularly, but I'm sure that's more complaining."

"What about Scott?" Ivy asked. "He admitted to having an affair."

"Yeah, he didn't bother hiding what he was doing," Brian said. "The secretary's name is Misty Frank and she's twenty-one and a bit of a scatterbrain. She posts selfies all over her Facebook page and Scott is in half of them. She calls him her 'sugar daddy' in almost every post."

"What an idiot," Jack muttered. "How about similar victims?"

"You and I both know that the Detroit area is far too big – and crime laden – to be able to pin down a particular pattern in such a short amount of time," Brian said. "If Scott is murdering there, I haven't been able to uncover it."

"Okay," Jack said, resting his chin on Ivy's shoulder. "What about Donnie?"

"Donnie lives north of Detroit, but still close enough to meet Scott for drinks every two weeks or so," Brian replied. "He works as an accountant for a middling firm. He makes middle five figures and doesn't appear to live above his means."

"Anything else?"

"He seems ... quiet," Brian said. "That could be a good thing or a bad thing. He did make one big purchase about a month ago. It's a diamond ring."

"I guess that means he's going to propose to Lauren after all," Ivy mused.

"I guess," Jack said. "You didn't find any relationships he was trying to hide, did you?"

"No," Brian answered. "He doesn't seem to be cheating on his girlfriend. He does have an unfortunate fantasy football habit, but I know a lot of guys who have the same problem and he's only losing a hundred bucks a week at most. He's not going broke, although he doesn't have a lot of savings."

"He lives in Rochester," Jack said. "Have you been able to track down similar murders there?"

"Again, that area is so populated I haven't had enough to time to really delve into it," Brian said. "I have feelers out, but so far I haven't found any murdered teenage girls."

"That leaves Alex," Jack said.

"Alex lives in Bay City and works as corporate finance manager," Brian said. "You probably already know that. His information is ... all over the place."

"Meaning?"

"For starters, he's in therapy with his wife once a week," Brian supplied. "I have no idea what they're talking about, but it's been going on for five months. Did you know their marriage was in trouble, too?"

"Not specifically, but it doesn't surprise me," Jack said. "What does surprise me is that Alex would go to therapy. He's never struck me as a big talker."

"Maybe Maria made an ultimatum," Ivy said. "If they are going to therapy, though, it doesn't seem to be working. They barely talk to one another."

"They don't openly fight either," Jack pointed out.

"I think that fighting is a better sign of a healthy relationship than not fighting," Ivy countered. "At least when you fight you know that there's enough passion to be angry at someone. Alex and Maria appear indifferent to one another. Not fighting is worse than fighting in some cases."

"Is that why we fight so much?" Jack asked. "Is it all the passion?"

"Why else do you think you jump me whenever we argue?"

"All right," Brian intoned, making a disgusted sound in the back of his throat. "That will be just about enough of that."

"Sorry," Jack said, smirking. "What else did you get on Alex?"

"Not much," Brian said. "He seems to keep to himself. There are no arrest reports or nuisance complaints from neighbors. Bay City is also small enough we would hear about dead teenagers, and they don't have any that match our criteria. In fact, the only teenage girl to die from something other than natural causes in that area over the past three years was in a car accident."

"What about the college?" Ivy asked.

"Bay City Community College?" Brian asked, furrowing his brow. "I didn't think to check with them, but the campus isn't big enough that they would be able to get away with their own internal investigation and not involve outside law enforcement."

"Not *that* college," Ivy clarified. "What about Central Michigan University? It's only about forty minutes away. That's not a huge distance when you're trying to cover your tracks, and that campus would be teeming with thousands of girls who are young enough to pique our killer's interest."

"Sometimes I think you missed your calling, Ivy," Brian said, chuckling. "I didn't think of that, but you're right on the money. I'll place a call to the Mount Pleasant Police Department and campus security. I don't suppose you want to join the force with Jack and me and solve crimes on a regular basis, do you?"

"I don't think my relationship with Jack could survive that much togetherness," Ivy teased, earning a squeeze from Jack.

"I think it's a great idea," Jack said. "I could be your boss, honey. Think of all the fun we could have."

"In your dreams," Ivy said. "I would be your boss."

"Well, that would be fun, too."

"I'm sorry I couldn't be more help," Brian said. "I'll check on the Central Michigan University angle and get back to you. What are you going to do?"

"I don't know what we're going to do, but I've decided that no matter what happens this is our last night staying at the campground," Jack said. "The more the noose tightens, the more desperate our killer is going to get. I'm starting to feel ... uneasy."

"I thought you wanted everyone to stay," Ivy said. "Why did you change your mind?"

"Because whoever killed Melissa went to a lot of trouble to make sure her body wouldn't be discovered," Jack replied. "Not only was it discovered, but you're the one who did it again. Someone is going to start looking at you as a mighty big threat after tonight. I can't have that."

"But ... ."

Jack cut her off with a curt shake of his head. "No. We either figure out who the guilty party is tonight or leave it for the state police. I won't risk you."

"I think that's a solid plan of action," Brian said, winking. "Be thankful that he cares enough about you to protect you at all costs, Ivy. That's a good thing. You two be careful, and I'll be in touch."

"Thank you."

BY THE TIME TROOPER HARVEY JOINED IVY AND JACK TWENTY minutes later, everyone was ready to put all of their cards on the table.

"Do you want to explain to me how you found this one?" Harvey asked.

"Ivy thought the kayaks would be a good way to dispose of a body because they were located so close to our campsite," Jack explained. "We both agreed that dumping blood in the clearing was an attempt to distract law enforcement. We decided to go out on the lake and see if we could figure out where Melissa's body was dumped."

"How did you happen upon the old summer camp?"

"I recognized it from when I was a kid," Ivy answered. "The east and west sides of the lake were too cluttered with houses. That would've been a huge risk. That left the summer camp, and it's been in the news because of that land development thing so I knew it was empty."

"Well, you're either incredibly intuitive or unbelievably lucky," Harvey said. "Either way, the coroner is putting Melissa Graham's death at between midnight and 2 a.m. on the evening she disappeared. We'll have a better number tomorrow."

"Are you going to make an arrest?" Jack asked.

"We don't have enough evidence to make an arrest," Harvey said. "We're leaning toward the husband for obvious reasons, but we can't rule out your other two friends and no one wants to jump the gun and arrest the wrong man."

"We're going back to the campground tonight," Jack said. "We're leaving tomorrow, though. I don't feel comfortable staying when I know that Ivy is going to be a target. I do have an idea about how we can make all of this come to a head tonight, though. If you're interested, that is."

Harvey leaned back in his chair, steepling his fingers on his chest and narrowing his eyes as he regarded Jack. "I'm listening."

"I know how to smoke our killer out."

Twenty-Three

"You know exactly what we're doing tonight, right?" Jack kept his voice low as he walked back to the campground with Ivy. "We can't afford any mistakes."

"We've been over the plan fifty times, Jack," Ivy said, her blue eyes alert. "I promise I'll follow your instructions. Don't worry about me."

"If I was capable of going through life not worrying about you we wouldn't be together," Jack shot back. "I'm going to lose a friend tonight any way you look at it. I might lose all of them. I find that I don't really care about that. I definitely care about losing you, though."

"You're very sweet."

"I'm being serious."

"Jack, I promise I will do exactly what we discussed," Ivy said. "Focus on what we have to do and not what you're worried I may do. I won't screw this up."

"Honey, I'm not worried about you screwing it up," Jack said, lifting their linked hands and pressing a soft kiss to Ivy's knuckles. "I'm worried we missed something and you'll end up in danger. I need you to be vigilant."

"Of course I'm going to be vigilant," Ivy said. "I can't miss the massage you're going to give me the minute we get home. That would be criminal."

"You're massaging me first."

"Maybe we can figure out a way to massage each other," Ivy suggested.

"We do that every night," Jack snickered, causing Ivy to blush. "You're massaging the heck out of me when this is over. You can't back out. I want lotions and the whole bit."

"If this plan works out, I'll do the massage naked," Ivy whispered.

"You are absolutely my favorite person in the world," Jack said, dropping a hot kiss on Ivy's lips as they approached their campsite. "Keep your eyes open, honey. This is about to get hairy."

Maria was the first to notice Jack and Ivy's arrival, and she didn't look happy to see them. "It's about time," she snapped. "You've been gone all day. You insisted that we stay even though it's dangerous, and then you took off and went on a romantic picnic. What do you have to say for yourself?"

"You're not my mother and I don't have to explain my actions," Jack replied. "We haven't been having a romantic picnic, though. In case you didn't notice, we took off on kayaks when we left this morning and we're walking back. Would you care to know why that is?"

Maria's face shifted from accusatory to worried. "What happened?"

"Gather everyone together around the fire," Jack instructed. "I have some bad news."

It took Maria less than five minutes to collect everyone, and once the five-member group was settled in chairs Jack took the opportunity to study the familiar faces he'd known for so long. He was convinced one of them was a killer. Now it was time to find out which one.

Scott was the first to speak, and although he looked miserable and sick, his voice was strong. "What's going on? Did you find information about Melissa?"

"Melissa is dead," Jack said, going for a dramatic announcement rather than a soft sell. "Her body was discovered on the other side of the lake this afternoon."

"What?" Lauren was horrified, her hand flying to her mouth. "How ... why ... when ... but ... ."

"She was killed the night she disappeared," Jack supplied. "The coroner believes she was struck over the head and transported to a summer camp on the opposite side of the lake. She was then stabbed in a neck so the killer could collect her blood and her body was dumped in a shack on the property."

"But ... why?" Donnie asked, his face plaintive.

"I can't give you all of the answers you're looking for right now," Jack said. "We don't know why anyone would go after Melissa. I have a lot to talk to you guys about, so everyone needs to prepare themselves for a really long discussion.

"First off, the police are aware of your financial problems, Scott," he continued. "They know about the life insurance policy and they know that you're about to go bankrupt. There's no sense lying about any of that when they get here to question you."

"And when will that be?" Alex asked. "Shouldn't he have a lawyer?"

"They should be here in about an hour," Jack replied. "If he needs a lawyer, he should definitely get one. That's not my business."

"How was Melissa's body discovered?" Lauren asked. "Did kids find it in the shack?"

"The summer camp is not in operation," Jack replied. "It's for sale and there's a fight between a land developer and the neighbors, so the body could've conceivably gone undiscovered for a long time."

"Who found it?" Maria asked.

"We did," Jack said, resting his hand on Ivy's knee. "Ivy went to the camp when she was a kid and was familiar with the unrest regarding it, so it made sense to check it out."

"It made sense?" Alex arched a dubious eyebrow. "How did it make sense? You said Melissa's blood was discovered close to where the first body was dumped. Why wouldn't you focus your search there?"

"Because police dogs scoured that entire area yesterday, and if there was a body close to that location they would've found it," Jack replied, locking gazes with Alex. "It was pretty obvious that the blood was dumped in the clearing as a forensic countermove. Once we knew that, the next step was to discover where Melissa's body was really discarded."

"I don't want to be the only jackass of the group, but have we considered that perhaps Ivy is the culprit?" Donnie asked. "No offense, Ivy. You're smoking hot and you seem nice. You also discovered three bodies. That can't be a coincidence."

"I agree with Donnie," Maria said. "Ivy is the newest face. We didn't have problems with our friends going missing – and being murdered – until she came along."

Jack was expecting the attack. "Ivy has already been cleared," he said. "She has an alibi for when the first victim went missing. She's also not strong enough to carry a dead body to a kayak, paddle it across the lake, and then carry it into a shack. Besides that, she was with me when both Kylie and Melissa went missing. As far as alibis go, that's a pretty good one."

"Maybe she had help," Scott suggested. "Maybe that werewolf guy she found in the woods is her partner and they've been doing it together. What did Melissa ever do to you?"

"I think you all know I'm not a killer," Ivy replied, refusing to get upset. Jack warned her that they would turn on her. "Besides, I don't have a motive."

"Who here has a motive for all three of these murders?" Lauren challenged. "I'll tell you who. No one."

"I have no idea who has a motive for all three murders," Jack said. "When we catch the killer, we'll have a better idea about motives. Whoever killed the two teenagers is obviously a sexual sadist. As for Melissa, maybe she discovered who the killer was and he had to shut her up. We just don't know."

"I thought you said the state police didn't give you any information on the second body you found?" Alex pressed. "Are they going public now? And if it was just bones, how can they be sure there was a sexual component?"

"I'm not privy to all their evidence, but they know exactly who the bones belong to," Jack said. "Her name was Hannah Gibson. She went missing almost exactly a year ago – when the six of you were here camping."

A hush fell over the group, everyone sucking in deep breaths as the reality of Jack's words rippled through the uneasy undercurrent washing over the campsite.

"How can they be sure?" Maria asked. "Just because she went missing when we were here ... ."

"Don't even float that theory," Jack chided. "We all know that you're grasping at straws. Someone here is a murderer. I don't suppose the guilty party would like to confess right now and save me invaluable time, would they?"

Five frightened gazes bounced around the circle. Jack couldn't ascertain if anyone was faking fear.

"You all have been putting on a show since we arrived," Jack said. "The police are scouring through all of your backgrounds even as we speak. Once they get the forensics back, then someone is going to prison for the rest of their life ... and the rest of us will never be the same."

"What do mean they've been going through our backgrounds?" Lauren asked. "How can they do that? That's an invasion of privacy."

"We have three dead bodies, Lauren," Jack countered. "Your privacy concerns don't mean squat to law enforcement. Do you want to know what they've already found out? I would love to tell you."

"I'm not sure that's necessary," Maria hedged.

Jack ignored her. "Let's start with Scott," he said. "We know Scott here has been seeing an idiotic girl named Misty Frank. She's barely out of her teens and refers to Scott as her 'sugar daddy' on Facebook. He didn't bother hiding his indiscretion.

"We also know that Scott is about to go belly-up financially," he continued. "Melissa had a shopping problem. By the way, Scott, if she was having an affair she was doing it with a disposable cell phone. The police have been all through her records, and with the exception of her book club and Maria, she didn't make regular calls to anyone."

Maria made a funny face that wasn't lost on Ivy. Instead of interrupting Jack when he was on a roll, though, Ivy filed it away for future reflection.

"Then there's Donnie," Jack said. "He seems to live a pretty clean life except for the fantasy football losses. He did buy a big ring about a month ago. I'm guessing that's for Lauren. I'm sorry if I ruined the proposal, but I'm sick of secrets."

"You bought me a ring?" Lauren's voice was soft. "Really?"

"I was going to propose in front of everyone on our last night here," Donnie admitted. "That changed after the Melissa thing, but … you know I love you. I don't want to lose you."

"Oh, that's so sweet," Lauren sighed.

"Yes, it's truly wonderful," Jack deadpanned. "Of course, he could be a murderer, so I would refrain from saying yes until we're sure he's in the clear."

"He's not a murderer and you know it," Lauren said, recovering her senses enough to unleash a new bout of anger on Jack. "What is wrong with you?"

"I'm nowhere near being done," Jack said, ignoring Lauren's outrage. "The police also know that Maria and Alex have been in therapy for months. It doesn't seem to be working. They barely acknowledge one another. Still, it's suspect.

"The good news for all of you is that local police departments close to where you live haven't been able to track down similar victims," he continued. "You're from heavily populated areas, though, and that's going to take more digging. They're also branching out to check Central Michigan University's unsolved crimes because of Alex's proximity to the campus."

"I'm glad to see you have so much faith in us," Alex said, his jaw clenched. "Did your partner betraying you and leaving you for dead make you lose faith in all humanity?"

"Or did you only lose faith in us?" Maria added.

"This has nothing to do with faith," Jack said. "Facts don't lie. Whoever grabbed Melissa was from this camp. It couldn't have been a woman working alone, and it's doubtful given the gossipy nature of this group a team could've gone undetected. That means the killer is a man.

"I know it's not me," he continued. "That leaves Donnie, Alex, and Scott."

"So, that's the way it is, huh?" Donnie asked, clasping his hands together on his lap. "You forged a new life and forgot your friends from your old one? Is that how you can see us as killers?"

"I don't want to see any of you as killers," Jack countered. "I can't ignore the evidence, though."

"You said that you were waiting on forensics," Alex said. "What does that mean?"

"Oh, whoever killed Melissa left a mountain of DNA evidence on her," Jack supplied. "They're rushing it through the lab. The state trooper we've been dealing with hopes to have a match by the time he gets here."

"But how?" Alex pressed. "You need to compare DNA against other DNA to get a match."

"Ivy and I collected DNA from everyone yesterday," Jack explained. It was a calculated lie, and it was the second part of his plan. "We got it from your hair brushes and shoulders when you weren't looking and bagged it in our tent."

"You're trying to set us up!" Lauren said, her legs shaking as she climbed to her feet and wagged an accusatory finger in Jack's face. "Ivy is doing this to clear herself and throw one of us under the bus."

"I guess we'll find out very soon," Jack said, leaning back in his chair and crossing his arms over his chest. "It shouldn't take long to finish the comparisons. As soon as it's done, we'll know who the guilty party is and they'll be arrested."

Scott jumped up from his chair, kicking it in Jack's direction as he made his move. "I'm not going to jail!" He broke into a run, racing away from the campsite. Jack had his answer, although he couldn't help but feel a little sorry about the outcome.

"Stay here, Ivy," Jack warned, hopping to his feet. "You know what to do."

Ivy watched as Jack tore off into the dwindling light. There was no way Scott could outrun him. It was almost over.

"I CAN'T BELIEVE THAT JUST HAPPENED," MARIA SAID, HER mouth hanging open. "I just can't believe it was Scott."

"Why not?" Lauren argued. "It made sense for him to be guilty. Why else go after Melissa? We all should've seen it."

Ivy internally rolled her eyes. She couldn't wait to be away from these people.

"What do you think will happen when Jack catches up to him?" Donnie asked, his eyes wide. "He won't kill him, will he?"

"Jack won't kill him," Ivy said. "Scott isn't a physical threat. Unless he's carrying a knife that no one saw – which I guess is possible because he had to have a weapon when he slaughtered Melissa – Jack will probably only tackle and cuff him."

"Hey, um … I'm sorry we accused you." Lauren said the words, but Ivy could tell she didn't mean them. "You're the newbie, though, so … ."

"It doesn't matter," Ivy said, pushing herself up from her chair. "This is going to be over soon. Come tomorrow, we'll probably never see each other again."

"Does that mean you're going to keep Jack away from us?" Maria asked.

"I would never keep Jack away from anyone," Ivy clarified. "If he wants to see you, he's more than welcome to visit. If I never see you people again, though, it will be too soon."

"You've got a charming personality," Lauren deadpanned.

"Right back at you."

The sun was fading, causing a chill to move through the air. Ivy ambled over to her tent to retrieve a hoodie, hoping it wouldn't be too long before Jack returned. She was dying to be present for Scott's confession, and Jack promised he would retrieve her before heading toward the state trooper station. They expected the guilty party to run. Ivy's only job was to remain behind and keep out of trouble.

Ivy leaned over to unzip the tent and felt a presence move in behind her. She could practically feel the menace wafting off of the interloper as he erased the distance between them. She opened her mouth to scream – or at least utter a hateful curse – but a hand clamped over her mouth before she had a chance.

It was only then that Ivy realized they'd made a mistake.

Twenty-Four

❦

Ivy fought her assailant, kicking out with her feet as she tried to connect with a knee or ankle, but whoever grabbed her was prepared for her efforts and managed to control them.

"Unless you want me to gut you right here, you're going to stop doing that," Alex hissed, his voice low and menacing. "I have nothing left to lose, Ivy. I will kill you if you fight me."

Ivy lowered her eyes, resigned. She made her body go limp as Alex moved to drag her into the woods. There were different ways to fight, and this was the only one that came to mind.

"Stop doing that," Alex muttered, his tone threatening as he fruitlessly tried to get Ivy to stand on two legs. "You're really starting to piss me off."

Ivy pretended to be boneless, forcing Alex to grip her with two hands as he toiled to carry her into the trees. She knew it wasn't much of a delay tactic, but she didn't have a lot of options.

It took Alex almost a full five minutes to drag Ivy far enough into the woods that he could speak without lowering his voice. He gave up trying to force her farther away from civilization at that point and finally threw her onto the ground with all of his might.

Ivy rolled to a sitting position, her eyes glittering with mayhem as she looked Alex up and down. He appeared to have become unhinged, a jagged-edged knife clutched in his hand. She didn't blame him for losing his notorious cool. He was about to go to prison for the rest of his life. The pacing and sputtering man running a hand through his dark hair was a far cry from the one Ivy was introduced to at the beginning of the week.

"I guess it's you, huh?" Ivy rubbed her sore hip. "Jack is going to kill you. You know that, right?"

"Oh, shut up!" Alex seethed. "This is all your fault. None of this would've ever happened if you'd kept your stupid nose out of our business."

"I think an argument could be made that none of this would've ever happened if you hadn't killed people," Ivy countered. "I think blaming me for your deficiencies is a surefire way to victimhood. I expected more from you."

Alex lashed out, backhanding Ivy across the face and causing her to cry out. "I don't think you understand your situation here, Ivy. You've ruined my life. Now I'm going to end yours. I would seriously rethink my attitude if I were you."

"You're not me."

"No, I'm not," Alex agreed. "I am going to use and abuse you before I put you out of your misery, though. You're my last chance at infamy. I guess I'd better make this one count, huh?"

JACK TACKLED SCOTT FROM THE SIDE, TAKING HIS FORMER friend by surprise when he popped out from behind a tree. Scott wasn't exactly known for his athletic prowess, so the fact that Jack not only managed to catch up to his old college roommate – but get ahead of him, too – wasn't a big surprise.

Scott hit the ground hard, gasping as the oxygen vacated his lungs.

"I can't say I'm not disappointed, Scott," Jack muttered, rolling the prone man onto his stomach so he could cuff his hands behind his back. "I was hoping it wasn't you. I didn't think anyone could be that stupid, but I guess I was wrong."

"I didn't kill her," Scott sputtered, whimpering as Jack pushed him to a sitting position. "I swear I didn't kill my wife. You have to believe me."

"Why would I believe you?" Jack challenged. "You ran when I told you about the forensic evidence. An innocent man wouldn't do that."

"Do you have him?" Harvey approached out of the darkness, three uniformed troopers flanking him. He had his gun drawn and an excited look on his face. "So it was the husband after all. I guess that figures."

"I didn't kill Melissa!" Scott howled. "Please, Jack, if our friendship ever meant anything to you … ."

"Scott, you ran," Jack exploded. "Why else would you run?"

"Because the forensic guys are going to find my … stuff … inside of Melissa when they do the autopsy," Scott said. "We had sex in the trailer that night. We got in an argument – like we always did – and it just sort of happened."

"It's convenient that you're just mentioning it now," Harvey pointed out.

"If you two agreed to divorce, why would you be having sex?" Jack asked.

Scott shrugged. "We were bored and didn't have anything better to do," he said. "After the argument … well … we were both keyed up. I only ran because I knew that the police would think I was guilty when the realized we had sex. I didn't kill her, though. You know I don't have it in me."

Right up until he bolted from his chair, Jack would've agreed with Scott. Now he wasn't so sure. "If you didn't do it, Scott, who did?"

"I don't know," Scott replied, angry. "I know it wasn't me. I want a lawyer."

"You can have one," Harvey said, retrieving Scott from the ground and handing him off to the troopers. "Read him his rights and transport him to the station." Harvey waited until Scott was out of earshot until he fixed his sympathetic eyes on Jack. "I'm sorry. I know he was your friend."

"I'm starting to wonder if any of them were every really my friends," Jack admitted. "I'm not bothered by you arresting him. If that's what you're worried about, don't."

"What is bothering you?"

"I never pegged Scott as being capable of murder," he said. "He's apparently an idiot and a philanderer, but I just can't reconcile that man being in good enough shape to carry Melissa's dead weight."

"Do you think he's telling the truth?" Harvey asked. "He might have panicked about the semen and made a boneheaded move. I've seen stranger things."

"I don't know," Jack replied. "I ... ." His heart rolled when Ivy's face popped into his head. "We need to get back to the campsite."

"Why?"

"Because if Scott is telling the truth, I just left my girlfriend alone with a murderer who has absolutely nothing to lose."

"HOW MANY TEENAGE GIRLS HAVE YOU KILLED?" IVY ASKED. She was stalling for time, hoping Alex would be happy to crow about his accomplishments. If she held on long enough, either Jack would find her or she'd discover a way out of this situation on her own.

"Eight," Alex replied. He didn't even need a moment to think about it.

"Who was your first victim?"

"Oh, that was a girl from college," Alex said, smiling at the memory. "Her name was Sydney Armstrong."

Ivy knit her eyebrows together. "Why does that name sound familiar?"

"Because that was the girl Jack had a crush on back in the day," Alex answered. "Don't you remember? We started talking about her during our hike – and I was really disappointed when the conversation shifted to you and your ex-boyfriend. I wanted to relive her death through Jack's misery, but you stole that from me."

"What happened with her?"

"Well, from Jack's perspective he was besotted with her and followed her around like a lost puppy dog," Alex said, his disdain for Jack obvious. "It was a mystery when she disappeared on her way home from the bar one night. It was a media circus for a week when no one could find a hint of what happened to her. It was a legend when no one found her body."

"Where is she?"

"I dumped her down an old well in the woods close to the dorms," Alex replied. "To my knowledge, she's never been found."

"How nice of you."

"It was an accident really," Alex said. "I wanted sex and she didn't want to give it up. I was dying to tell Jack I nailed her because I knew it would crush him. Do you have any idea how annoying it was to pal around with Jack? Women flocked to him. He was the hot one and the rest of us ... well ... the rest of us were just his lesser friends."

"Is that your excuse?" Ivy scoffed. "Are you going to blame being a sociopath on Jack?"

"I'm not a sociopath, Ivy," Alex countered. "I'm a psychopath. I feel love and desire. I'm not great with guilt. I do feel emotions, though. I just like the killing. I fought the urge for years. Each time I killed I told myself it would be the last time. Finally, I just realized I am who I am and embraced my true self."

"You're so ... sick," Ivy said, disgusted. "How did you get your hands on Hannah Gibson?"

"Oh, she looked like an angel," Alex intoned. "She had long blond hair and bright blue eyes. They were almost as pretty as yours. She was angry about having to go camping with her parents. When she snuck out to meet up with some teenagers she met earlier in the day – I was watching her so I knew exactly what she was planning – I grabbed her off the trail.

"I knocked her out because I was worried about people over-hearing us," he continued. "She was heavy for a tiny girl, but I knew about the clearing because I found it during a walk earlier. I knew it was far enough away to have fun, and remote enough to let her scream without detection."

"She wasn't found in the clearing, though," Ivy pointed out.

"No. She was raped there, though," Alex said. "I thought she was down for the count. She'd been whimpering throughout our ... date ... but she'd gone quiet. Imagine my surprise when she took off running."

"You chased her to that area," Ivy surmised. "Then you killed her there and didn't want to bother dragging her back to the clearing."

"It was a remote environment and as good a place as any to rid myself of her," Alex said. "It worked, too. No one found her for an entire year. I think she would've gone undiscovered forever – just like Sydney – if it wasn't for you."

"Why would you risk taking Kylie Bradford when you knew Jack was sharing the same campground?" Ivy asked. "You were just asking for trouble."

"I couldn't help myself," Alex replied. "She was just so cute. Plus, the idea of killing someone under Jack's nose was too glorious to ignore. He's always so full of himself. I followed you earlier that day to the clearing. I was hoping you two were going to do it right there so I could get another glimpse of you without your clothes on. I thought it was somehow ... poetic ... to finish what I started the previous year in such an ideal location."

"Why did you mutilate her? Did you do that to all of your victims?"

"That was my first time doing that," Alex said. "It just kind of occurred to me that it would be fun. I also thought I might be able to make it look like animals ripped her apart. She wasn't out there long enough for that, though. Thanks to you again, of course."

"You're welcome."

"I am dying to know how you found Melissa," Alex said, cocking an eyebrow. "Do you want to share with the class how you managed to do all of that?"

"Sure," Ivy said, tamping down her terror. "Have a seat and I'll tell you a story."

"DID you catch Scott?" Donnie asked, rising from his chair when he saw Jack and Harvey approach.

"I did," Jack replied, scanning the campsite. "Where is Ivy?"

No one answered his question.

"Did he admit to killing Melissa?" Maria asked.

"Did he say why he did it?" Lauren chimed in.

"Where is Ivy?" Jack bellowed.

The women looked taken aback.

"I don't know," Maria replied. "The last time I saw her she was heading toward your tent."

"How long ago was that?" Harvey asked, watching as Jack strode toward the tent and looked inside.

"About a twenty minutes ago," Maria replied.

"She not here," Jack said, growling as he took a second look around the campsite. "Where is Alex?"

"I ... ." Maria broke off, biting her lip. "He disappeared about the same time Ivy did."

"Son of a ... ."

"I'M A witch," Ivy announced, causing Alex's eyebrows to fly up his forehead. "It's the truth. I have powers and I can see things. That's how I knew how to find all three bodies."

"You're a witch?" Alex looked dubious.

"I am," Ivy said. "I can see things associated with death. It's a ... gift." Ivy had no idea if Alex believed her lie. She was trying to keep him engaged in the conversation long enough to formulate an escape plan. She had no idea what else to do.

"You're full of crap."

"Fine, I'm full of crap," Ivy said. "How else do you explain me finding three bodies in less than a week?"

"I have no idea," Alex shot back. "I have a feeling you'll tell me before I'm done with you, though." He made a move to approach her and Ivy scooted back to maintain distance between them. She didn't want to panic, but she was getting perilously close to falling apart.

"You haven't told me why you killed Melissa yet," Ivy gritted out. "Did she figure out what you were doing?"

"You're a curious little thing, aren't you?"

"I want to know all the answers before I die," Ivy said. "I think I've earned it."

"Fine," Alex said, letting loose with an exaggerated sigh. "If you must know, Melissa and I have been sleeping together for the past year. There. Are you satisfied?"

Ivy knit her eyebrows together, confused. "The phone calls."

"What phone calls?"

"The police went through Melissa's phone records," Ivy said. "They assumed she was talking to Maria when she called your house. She wasn't, though. She was talking to you. That's why Maria was so confused when Jack mentioned it earlier tonight."

"Melissa was excessively needy," Alex said. "She was determined to get me to leave Maria for her. She thought she could take the money from her divorce and we could move someplace else and get some house she desperately wanted. She was an idiot."

"You were sleeping with Melissa for a year," Ivy said, mostly talking to herself. "That means you started sleeping with her during your camping trip last year. Did she catch you killing Hannah?"

"She caught me coming out of the woods after killing Hannah," Alex clarified. "She asked a lot of questions, so I had to distract her. After chasing Hannah through the woods, I was kind of amped up and I couldn't risk Hannah getting away again so I had to kill her before we could have another round of fun. I settled for getting down and dirty with Melissa in the woods.

"Unfortunately, she assumed that meant we were going to be mated for life," he continued. "I had to set up meetings so we could do it as often as possible. I knew she would tell Maria if I didn't capitulate to her demands. It was really annoying."

"Melissa figured it out, didn't she?" Ivy pressed. "That's why you killed her."

"Yes," Alex confirmed. "She had sex with her husband in the trailer and then met me in the woods for our scheduled rendezvous. I could smell Scott on her. Now, I didn't want that woman, but the idea that she would touch that loser when she was supposed to be meeting me was too much to take.

"I called her a whore and she took it personally," he continued. "Then she told me that she knew I was the one who killed Kylie. She followed me that night."

"Why didn't she say something?"

"And blow her perfect façade out of the water?" Alex snorted. "You're giving Melissa way too much credit. She wanted me to give her money to keep her mouth shut instead. She was an idiot."

"So, what? You hit her over the head and dragged her down to a kayak?"

"I used my belt to hook her hands and ankles over the sides of the kayak, securing them underneath so she had nowhere to go, and paddled her over to the camp," Alex supplied. "We had a couple hours of fun there. She screamed a lot. Then I stabbed her in the neck and collected her blood. I knew you would check the clearing first. I figured you would waste time looking for Melissa there and no one would ever discover her body at the camp."

"I guess it sucks to be you," Ivy said. "Now your whole plan is smoked."

"All thanks to you," Alex said. "I knew tonight that Jack was going to catch me. Scott took off like an idiot and bought me some time, but there's no way Jack will believe he's capable of murder once he talks to him."

"I had a choice, I could run or I could stay behind and have one more bout of fun," he said. "I opted for the fun ... and you."

"You probably should've chosen to run," Jack said, a gun in his hand as he moved into the clearing.

Ivy sighed, relieved. "Jack."

"I'm right here, honey," Jack said, keeping the gun trained on Alex as his longtime friend debated his options.

Alex clutched the knife tighter and focused on Jack. "How did you find us?"

"Andrew Devlin saw you drag Ivy into the woods and met us on the trail by the campsite," Jack replied. "He knew exactly where you were."

"The werewolf strikes again," Alex muttered. "Where is Scott?"

"In custody."

"How did you know it was me?" Now Alex was the one buying time.

"I just had a feeling Scott wasn't capable of murder," Jack answered. "When both you and Ivy were gone from the campsite, I knew it was you. You've always been jealous. The only play that would make any sense for you is to try and take her out to punish me."

"You should've died when your partner shot you, Jack," Alex intoned. "You deserved it. Instead, you clung to life and … got everything you ever wanted. It's unbelievable how you luck into things."

"Step away from Ivy," Jack ordered, gesturing with his gun.

"Do you think you can shoot me in time to keep me from stabbing her, Jack?" Alex asked. "I'm kind of interested to see if you can."

"If you move toward her, I will kill you," Jack said.

"I want to die, Jack," Alex said. "We both know I'm not going to do well in prison."

"Don't move toward that woman," Harvey ordered, stepping into the small area behind Alex and splitting his attention.

"Oh, wow, that was smart," Alex said. "You brought help. You wanted to make sure your precious Ivy was safe. She's smart and pretty, Jack. You made a good choice."

"I know," Jack replied, his tone deadly. "Don't make me kill you, Alex. You can live out the rest of your days in prison. You owe some parents a few answers. Do the right thing for once in your life."

"I don't think so," Alex said, adjusting his grip on the knife. "I think I want to take my chances instead. I think I can get to Ivy and slit her throat before you shoot me. If I do, I win. If you shoot me before I get to her, I win. Either way … I win."

Alex didn't wait for Jack to respond, instead taking advantage of the lull in the conversation and lunging toward Ivy. Jack was ready for the move and he pulled the trigger without blinking an eye.

Ivy gasped as she covered her head, swiveling quickly when Alex's lifeless body fell at her feet. She scrambled to a standing position and bolted in Jack's direction. He caught her in mid-air, clutching her close.

"No," he whispered into her hair. "I win."

Twenty-Five

❧❧❧

"I knew you would find me," Ivy said two hours later, accepting a cup of hot chocolate from Jack in one of the conference rooms at the state police outpost. She'd just finished being debriefed for what felt like forever.

"I wouldn't have been able to find you if it wasn't for Andrew," Jack said, rubbing the back of her head. "I'm sorry I left you."

"You couldn't have known that would happen, Jack," Ivy chided. "I didn't see it coming either. When Scott took off like that … ."

"In my heart, I knew Scott wasn't capable of murder," Jack argued. "He was an idiot … and disloyal … and altogether moronic in some instances, but he wasn't a murderer."

"Alex has been killing a long time," Ivy said, resting her head against Jack's chest. "He killed the girl you had a crush on in college."

"I heard your statement to Harvey," Jack said, idly running his fingers up Ivy's spine. "Harvey is going to send searchers out to the well tomorrow morning. At least Sydney will be at rest now."

"I'm sorry you had to kill your friend."

"I'm not," Jack said. "I'm glad I got to you in time."

Harvey joined the couple a few minutes later, his expression rueful. "We're cutting Scott loose and your other friends are here to collect him," he said. "They say they're leaving town right after and want to say goodbye to you."

"Tell them I said goodbye," Jack said. "Tell them I wish them well. I won't be going up there, though."

"Are you sure?" Ivy asked, her blue eyes conflicted as they searched his face. "They're your friends, Jack."

"I don't think they are," Jack replied. "Not any longer, honey. We're old acquaintances, and I have nothing to say to them. I don't want to see them ... not now, at least."

"I'll take care of it," Harvey said. "You should know that we're probably going to be in touch with you over the next few weeks as we try to sort out Alex's list of victims. We're also going to have to talk to his wife, and she doesn't seem thrilled with any of this."

"Did she suspect it was Alex?" Ivy asked.

"She says she didn't until Jack mentioned phone calls between Melissa and her house," Harvey answered. "She said she wasn't talking to Melissa. That meant it had to be Alex."

"We should've remembered that," Ivy said. "Maria told us that Melissa only came around when she was forced or wanted to brag. That was our clue and we missed it."

"We had a lot of clues to sift through, honey," Jack said, rocking Ivy slightly as he pressed a kiss to her forehead. "I'm not sure I believe Maria didn't suspect Alex. I guess it doesn't matter now."

"We'll sort it all out," Harvey said. "Why don't you guys get out of here. I would suggest checking into a hotel instead of returning to the campground. That place is probably filled with bad memories for you."

"Not all the memories are bad," Jack said. "Besides, if what you say is true, we'll have the campsite to ourselves. I think that sounds like the best thing to happen to us for this entire trip."

Harvey shook Jack's hand and offered Ivy a tight smile. "Good luck."

"You, too."

JACK AND IVY WERE ALMOST TO JACK'S TRUCK IN THE PARKING

lot when four faces moved into their path, forcing Jack to shift Ivy closer as his protective instincts took over.

"Jack," Donnie said, his voice small. "We were hoping to run into you before we left."

"I'm too tired for this," Jack said. "I don't want to have some deep discussion. I don't want to hear how you had no idea Alex was doing what he was doing. I am sorry I tackled you, Scott, but you kind of had it coming."

"What am I supposed to do now?" Scott asked.

"Go home."

"What about me?" Maria asked.

"You're going to have a lot of questions to answer, but then you can go home, too," Jack said, his voice devoid of warmth.

"What are you going to do?" Lauren asked, her gaze bouncing between Jack and Ivy. "Are you just going to walk away and never look back?"

"We're going back to camp to get some sleep," Jack said. "Then we're getting up early tomorrow morning and packing up our stuff. Then we're going back to Ivy's house where she's going to give me the best massage ever. Then we're going to go on with our lives."

"You forgot one thing," Ivy interjected.

"What?" Jack asked, confused.

"We have to stop out at Andrew's place so I can thank him for sending you after me," Ivy said.

"We definitely have to do that," Jack said.

"So, that's it?" Donnie pressed. "You're done with us?"

"I think you guys need to find out who you are and stop living lies," Jack answered. "You're never going to be happy as long as you're pretending to live one life while actually living another. Maybe we'll run into each other again down the road. Maybe it will be a happy occurrence. For now, I have the life I want ... and the woman I want. I have no interest in living a lie."

"I hope you all find happiness," Ivy offered, letting Jack lead her around his old friends and toward their future. "I hope when things settle down, you all figure out where you're supposed to be."

Jack opened Ivy's door and helped her into the cab of his truck, pressing a sweet kiss to her lips before risking a glance over his shoulder. His friends remained rooted to their spots, staring in their direction with morose looks on their faces. "They're lost."

"You're found, though," Ivy said, running her finger down his cheek.

"I definitely am," Jack said, giving her another kiss. "Do you want to pick up dinner on the way back to camp?"

"Let's just go to sleep," Ivy said. "I'll buy you breakfast on our way home tomorrow."

"At least we know things will be dull tonight," Jack said, chuckling. "I ... ." He didn't get a chance to finish his statement because a mournful howl filled the air and drowned out the rest of his response.

Ivy widened her eyes. "It's the dogman."

"You did that on purpose."

In the end, it didn't matter if the dogman was real. Everything about their relationship was, and that's all either of them cared about.

Made in the USA
Middletown, DE
22 November 2019